I0673440

## PRAISE FOR JAMES SCOTT BELL

James Scott Bell has produced gold in the Mike Romeo series, about a one-time cage fighter and certified genius on a quest for virtue. I want to be Mike Romeo when I get younger. Highly recommended.

— **LARS WALKER, BRANDYWINE BOOKS**

A master of the cliffhanger, creating scene after scene of mounting suspense and revelation . . . Heart-whamming.

— **PUBLISHERS WEEKLY**

There'll be no sleeping till after the story is over.

— **JOHN GILSTRAP**, NYT BESTSELLING AUTHOR

James Scott Bell's series is as sharp as a switchblade.

— **MEG GARDINER**, EDGAR AWARD WINNING AUTHOR

# ROMEO'S TRUTH

## JAMES SCOTT BELL

Compendium Press

Copyright © 2025 by James Scott Bell

All rights reserved.

No part of this book may be reproduced in any form or by any electronic or
mechanical means, including information storage and retrieval systems,
without written permission from the author, except for the use of brief
quotations in a book review.

This is a work of fiction. Names, characters, businesses, places, events,
locales, and incidents are either the products of the author's imagination or
used in a fictitious manner. Any resemblance to actual persons, living or
dead, or actual events is purely coincidental.

Compendium Press
Woodland Hills, CA

ISBN: 978-0-910355-66-7

# ROMEO'S TRUTH

In a time of deceit telling the truth is a revolutionary act.

— GEORGE ORWELL

Gussie's Diner was old school. The booths were upholstered in faded red vinyl and dull brass studs. The Formica counter had seen decades of spilled coffee, salt, ketchup, grease, bread crumbs, and elbows. There was a ticket spinner at the kitchen window. A lone ceiling fan pushed around the aroma of java, hamburgers and grilled onions.

Half a dozen customers were lunching. Four men in a booth looked like they spent a lot of time in the sun. A woman sat at a table, reading a book and drinking coffee. An older gent with arms baked to a rich brown chomped a sandwich at the counter.

A waitress showed me to a table by the window. It had a stunning view of the parking lot. She handed me a menu and asked if I'd like something to drink.

"Lemonade, please," I said.

With a nod, she left, and I turned to the bill of fare. It

majored in meat. Not only burgers, but New York strip, top sirloin, ribeye (boneless or bone-in), T-bone, and porterhouse.

When the waitress came back with my lemonade I said, "Good variety of cow."

"That's because you're in cow country," she said. She was around thirty. Her name badge read *Maria.*

"I passed a bunch of them a ways back," I said.

She nodded.

"Something wrong?" I said.

"Where you from?" she said.

"L.A."

"You didn't hear about the killings?"

"Killings?"

"Somebody poisoned five cows at the Rendell Ranch," she said. "That's what you passed."

"Whoa. They know who did it?"

She shook her head.

"Sorry to hear that," I said.

"What can I get you?"

"Give me another couple of minutes. I want to consult my taste buds."

She laughed and moved on.

I gave the menu some study. I got my choices down to the New York strip and the boneless ribeye. Since New York was going insane, I decided on the ribeye. You really can't go wrong with a ribeye. Especially in cattle country.

I took out my phone to search for the story about the poisoned cows. I found one on a site called The Central Valley Dispatch.

### Five Cows Poisoned on Local Ranch: Sheriff Investigates Possible Anti-Beef Link

by Jamie Anderson, Staff Writer

Five cows on the sprawling Rendell Ranch were discovered dead this week, from suspected poisoning. The incident has left the local community on edge and the sheriff's office scrambling for leads.

The cows, all healthy and in prime condition, were found lifeless in their pastures early Monday morning by ranch hands. Initial investigation suggests that the animals ingested a toxic substance, but authorities have yet to determine the exact poison used or how it was administered.

Sheriff Javier Cortez, leading the investigation, expressed his concern at a press conference yesterday. "This is a serious and troubling incident," he said. "At this point, we have no suspects, but we are exploring all possible avenues."

One potential motive the sheriff's office is considering involves anti-beef environmentalists. Over the past year, there has been a noticeable increase in protests and activities against cattle ranching, driven by concerns about the environmental impact of beef production. "We can't rule anything out," Sheriff Cortez said. "There are groups out there with strong feelings about the beef industry, and it's something we're looking into."

Local ranchers are understandably alarmed. Travis Rendell, owner of Rendell Ranch, spoke about the emotional and financial toll of the incident. "We care deeply about our livestock and the land," Rendell said. "We are committed to safety and quality control. This crime is devastating."

The sheriff's office is urging anyone with information about the incident to come forward. "We need the community's help," Sheriff Cortez said. "If anyone saw anything unusual or has any information that could assist our investigation, we ask that they contact us immediately."

I sipped some lemonade and looked at another story. It profiled a local woman named Grandma Pie because she baked

—wait for it—pies. Her specialty was Chess Pie, which she explained came from her Southern ancestors. "It's a simple recipe, so when folks asked what kind of pie it was, they'd say, 'It's just pie.' Only it sounded like 'jess pie.' So the folks called it Chess Pie."

Bless their hearts.

I heard tires screech. A red Toyota tore into the parking lot and burned to a stop. A black Chevy pickup shot in behind it.

The driver of the car got out. He was a wiry kid, late teens, dressed in shorts and a short-sleeved shirt.

The pickup guy was older, thick, about my height. Bald, reddish beard, big arms. Flannel shirt, jeans and cowboy boots.

He advanced on the kid, who had his arms out in a what's-up gesture.

Baldy walked up to him and said something.

The vibe was so hot I felt it through the window. I knew exactly what would happen next.

Baldy punched the kid in the face. The kid went down like a sack of broken glass.

I got up and ran out.

Baldy was leaning over, pummeling the kid's face. I grabbed the back of his shirt and pulled him up. He spun around and I shoved him. He stumbled backward. I stepped between him and the kid.

He took a second to size me up.

"You're in the wrong place," he said.

"You've done enough," I said.

"This ain't your business."

For some reason I quoted Marley's Ghost from *A Christmas Carol*. I do that sometimes. "Mankind is my business. Their common welfare is my business."

He asked me what kind of excrement that was.

"You can go now," I said.

"Ain't goin' nowhere," he said.

"You really should," I said. "You can still walk."

He smiled. "Big talk for a candy boy."

Candy boy? Because I was wearing a Hawaiian shirt with hibiscus and parrots? You can insult me, but not my shirts.

He balled his hands.

"You don't want to do that," I said. "Not in boots."

He squinted.

"You can't get good footing," I said.

He raised his fists.

I shook my head. "My wife doesn't like me to fight."

He snorted a laugh. It sounded like a bullfrog sneezing.

"You're just whipped," he said. "Do what little wifey says."

"First of all, she's not little," I said. "Almost six feet. Athletic, too. Played volleyball in college and—"

He spat two words.


Street fights usually end quick. If the guys are untrained, it gets ugly and wild punches are thrown until one lands. If a guy is big, like this goon, he's probably won a number of encounters and has it wired into his brain that he's cock of the walk, the rooster in the barnyard, the big dog. He has no plans or strategy. He depends on his muscles, not his mind.

You need both in a fight. Because adrenaline kicks in, flows to the brain, drowns out thought. Unless you're trained to know what to do with it.

Baldy wasn't trained.

I charged. He threw a wild right. I ducked it. I gave him an iron-fingers jab to his carotid. His eyes popped. He wobbled and sucked for air.

I finished him with a left to the temple. He kissed asphalt.

I attended to the kid. His face was red and blood trickled

from his nose. He was groggy. I helped him to his feet, put his arm around my shoulder and walked him into the diner.

I sat him in a booth. Maria came over, concern on her face.

"Get me a wet towel," I said.

"This is very bad," she said.

"Towel?"

She went for one.

The kid groaned.

"Easy, pal," I said. "We'll get you cleaned up."

Maria came back with the towel and I gently mopped his face.

"You better go," Maria said.

"Why?"

"Trust me. That man you fought with. He's bad."

"We need to report this," I said.

"Nothing will happen."

"What?"

"Just believe me. Get in your car and go."

"I don't take to running away," I said.

Maria looked out the window.

Baldy was up, shaking his head. He looked at us. Then got in his truck and took off.

"He'll be back," Maria said.

"Tell me what's going on," I said.

"Don't get involved," Maria said.

"I'm already involved."

The kid slid out of the booth, unsteady on his feet.

"I'm okay," he said, and started for the door.

"Wait," I said.

He didn't wait.

"You sure you can drive?" I said.

He went out the door and made for his car.

I turned to Maria. "Now can you tell me what this about?"

"You've got to go," she said.

"Not till I find out."

She gave me a look and knew I meant it.

She called to the other waitress. "Ruth, take over, okay?"

To me she said, "Hold on."

She went to the counter, took off her apron and stuffed it underneath. She came out with her purse.

W e went out to the lot. She told me to follow her car. I got in Spinoza, my classic Mustang. She led me down a couple of roads, through open land dotted with a few ranch-style houses.

We got to a dirt road and drove up to a little clapboard house. She stopped and got out and came over to my car.

"Who are you?" she asked.

"Name's Mike," I said. "I work for a lawyer in Los Angeles and there's a witness in Los Banos I need to interview. I was hungry and pulled off and found your diner."

"You found a lot more than that. The guy you fought with is Dante Hooker. He has a rep. And he has friends."

"Local punk?" I said.

"He's more than that," Maria said. "I think he's killed people."

"You know this?"

"Not for certain. I know he likes people to think that."

"An intimidator," I said.

"Something like that."

"Usually that means he's working for somebody."

"It really would be best for you to go on your way. There's nothing more you can do here."

"I'd like to know why he was beating up that kid," I said.

"There's no way to find out now," Maria said.

"There are always ways."

"What ways?"

"My ways."

She gave me a long, lingering look. I get that a lot.

I said, "What did you mean when you said it wouldn't matter if we called this in?"

"Just trust me on that," she said. "I've lived here all my life."

I looked at the house. "Here?"

"I live with my dad," she said. "He's in ill health."

"Where'd you go to college?" I asked.

She looked surprised. "Why do you think I went to college?"

"You said ill health. That bespeaks education."

"I went to UC Davis," she said.

"An aggie?"

She nodded. "What about you? Not many people say bespeaks."

"I'm embarrassed to say."

"Why?"

"Because the place has gone where handbaskets go."

"I think I know what you mean," she said. "But …"

"Yes?"

"The way you fought."

"I've had some experience in that line," I said.

"Maria!" An old man stood in the doorway.

Maria turned. "It's all right, Papito." Then to me, "My father."

Papito said something to her in Spanish.

"He's curious about who you are," Maria said.

"Understandable," I said.

"What do you want me to tell him?" she said.

"I'll tell him myself." I got out and walked with Maria to the house. The old man was short and stocky, had a weathered face with wispy hair on top. He eyed me with curiosity mixed with suspicion.

"Buenos días," I said, extending my hand.

He paused a moment, then shook. His grip was iron.

"You can speak English," he said.

"My name is Mike Romeo. I had a bite to eat at Gussie's and your daughter served me."

"He stopped a fight," Maria said. "With Dante."

Papito's eyes flashed. "Come inside. I want to hear."

Maria said, "Papito, he has business and needs to—"

"Would you like a beer?" Papito said.

"Love one," I said.

The living room had a comfortable, lived-in look. Not messy, but not pristine, either. On one wall were framed photographs. One of them was of a little girl holding a chicken. Another had a young man in an Army uniform, steely-eyed and leaning against a jeep. Surrounding foliage suggested Vietnam as the location.

Maria told her father to sit and put on his oxygen. He grunted and went to a chair. There was an oxygen tank on a roller by the chair. Papito shook his head as he put the plastic tubes in his nose.

"I have COD," he said.

"COPD," Maria said.

"Smoking is very bad," Papito said. "Maria, will you get the beer?"

Maria went to the kitchen.

"Please sit," Papito said.

I sat in the other chair.

"I want to know about this fight," Papito said.

"Just one of those things," I said. "I happened to be there when this guy called Dante started wailing on a smaller guy in the parking lot."

"You fought with him?"

"I just wanted to stop him," I said. "He outweighed the other guy by a hundred pounds, at least."

"You are a big guy," Papito said.

"I try to eat right."

"You are not from around here."

"Los Angeles," I said.

Maria came back with three cans of Tecate. She handed one to me and one to her father. She sat on the sofa with the third.

"I am from there," Papito said.

"He was a boy in Chavez Ravine," Maria said.

"Dodger Stadium," I said.

"Malo," Papito said. He took a swig of beer and banged the can on a side table like a judge's gavel.

"His family was displaced when they built the stadium," Maria said. "You know about that?'

"A little," I said.

"There was a Mexican community there. Poor families. The city took it over. Evicted everybody. They were going to build housing projects."

Papito grunted.

Maria said, "But then they sold the land to that man…"

"O'Malley!" Papito said.

"Who built a stadium instead. That's when the family came here."

I nodded.

"Why have you come?" Papito said. He had balled his hands into loose fists. I could read in those rough hands a lifetime of hardscrabble living and inner resolve to fight, no matter the odds. Good hands, the kind you want on your side when the chips are down.

"I work for a lawyer," I said. "We have a case coming up, and there's a witness I'm to interview in Los Banos."

Papito chortled.

"He calls it The Bathrooms," Maria said. "He knows better."

"Tell me more about the fight," Papito said.

"He doesn't need to do that," Maria said.

"I want to hear."

"It was just a short fight," I said.

"You know how to box?" Papito said.

"A little," I said.

"Why do you know?" he said.

Maria looked at me, as if to say I didn't need to go on. But I liked the old man.

"I did some fighting," I said. "For money."

"In the ring?"

"In cages, mostly."

"Do you still?" he said.

"Not formally," I said. "On occasion, in my line of work, it happens."

"Tell me about the fight."

"It wasn't much," I said. "The guy has no skills. I ducked his punch and gave him one in the throat, then decked him with my left."

Papito smiled. "I wanted to be a boxer. Do you know about Art Aragon?"

"I don't," I said.

"From Los Angeles. A great boxer. He was called The Golden Boy. There are many stories."

"I've heard them all," Maria said.

"He had many girls," Papito said. "Do you know of Jane Fields?"

"Jayne Mansfield," Maria said.

"Hubba hubba," Papito said. "Do you have a girl?"

"A wife," I said.

"What is her name?" he said.

"Sophie."

"Is she hubba hubba?"

"Three hubbas," I said.

Papito laughed. He told me some more of his background, mentioning Vietnam only once, and quickly. He happily recounted his move to central California where he married and started a family. Because of his Army training he knew his way around machinery, and got a job with one of the larger farms in the area, keeping tractors and a fleet of trucks in shape.

He wanted to know more about me, but he was starting to look tired. Maria told him I had work to do and they needed to let me go. I exchanged phone numbers with Maria. If she ever found out who the kid was, and how he was doing, she could give me a call.

Papito said I should come back again. He liked talking to me.

"Sure," I said, knowing I wouldn't be stopping here on my way back to home and Sophie.

How wrong I was.

I got on the 5 North. Spinoza hummed along, perhaps the way his namesake Baruch Spinoza hummed as he walked the streets of Amsterdam contemplating infinite substance. I passed a Walmart truck rumbling behind a Heinz truck with a big, red ketchup bottle painted on the side. In front of that was a plain white semi hauling *Valley Gold Produce*. The tagline was *Taste the Heart of California.*

When I got to a long stretch with no trucks and only a few distant cars in sight, I called Ira.

"How goes it, Michael?"

"Interesting question."

"Hoo boy," he said. That's his usual response when I'm cryptic. And I love being cryptic.

"I'm on my way to Los Banos," I said. "But I made a little stop."

"And?"

"I had what you might call an altercation."

Ira said nothing. I could just see him rubbing the bridge of his nose.

"Not a big one," I said. "There was a guy beating up another guy in the parking lot of this diner. I stopped him."

"How badly did you stop him?"

"Two punches," I said. "That's all. Not much to it. I'll tell you all about it later."

"I'd prefer it if you'd tell me now," Ira said. "I can't live with the suspense."

"Call it a mystery, then."

"Michael…"

"It's okay," I said. "Nobody's dead, if that's what you're thinking."

"I should count my blessings."

"I did the minimum amount of damage to stop a big guy putting real hurt on a small guy," I said.

"And what is the fallout?" Ira said.

"Nothing that I can see. I'm off to do my professional duty."

"Good. Stick to it and then come home."

"Miss me?" I said.

Pause. "Let's just say you keep life interesting."


I called Sophie.

"Hello, Romeo," Sophie said.

"I'm calling from lovely Highway 5, heading to Los Banos."

"How's the trip been?"

"Interesting," I said.

"Uh-oh." That's Sophie's version of Ira's "Hoo boy."

"Not too much uh-oh," I said.

"How much?" she said.

"Half a cup. I had to break up a fight."

"How bad is the other guy?"

"He was down for a while, but left under his own power."

"Want to tell me about it?" Sophie said.

"Can it wait till I get home?"

"Now I'm really curious."

"You sound like Ira," I said.

"I should be so wise," she said.

"How are things at the Cove?"

"All's well," Sophie said. "C Dog came over for a bit and talked to me about his new girlfriend. He said he doesn't understand women."

"Can you blame him?" I said.

"I'll ignore that," she said. "When will you be back?"

"I'll spend the night at a motel. Then home."

"I'll make you chile rellenos."

"After you flood me with kisses?"

"A lot more than that," she said.

I pushed hard on the gas pedal.

L os Banos is a town stuck between worlds, a place where weathered storefronts and sun-bleached signs meet the hopeful green of parks and rec. Dry open spaces and strip malls, cracked asphalt roads and fast-food chains. Quiet and stubborn, like an old prospector with a new pan. The air was redolent with the scent of cattle and alfalfa.

I found the house in a residential section where Spanish tile roofs were the preferred design. This house had a gnarly wood fence on the sides. A couple of shaggy cyprus trees did guard duty in the dirt of the front yard.

I knocked on the door. Waited. Knocked again. I sensed the silence of suspicion inside.

A voice said, "Yes, please?"

"Mrs. Ramirez?"

"Who is it?"

"My name is Mike Romeo, I work for a lawyer in Los Angeles."

Silence.

"It's very important that I talk to you," I said. "May I come in?"

"I do not know who you are."

"Let me give you a card."

"I do not want to talk about it."

"Please, Mrs. Ramirez. Just a few minutes."

"Please go now. I'm sorry. But please."

Now what? I wasn't going to force my way in. She didn't have to talk to me. I thought I'd gain a little sympathy for the long drive. But she was clearly afraid.

"Mrs. Ramirez, we represent the man accused of the shooting. You may be our only witness."

"I don't want to be," she said.

"Are you afraid of the gangs?"

"Yes."

A common problem. Both witnesses and potential jurors afraid to be involved in a gang related case. Afraid of retaliation, intimidation, their family members getting threats.

"May I show you one picture then?" I said. "You can at least help us focus our attention."

"Will I have to talk in court?"

We could always subpoena her, but that is ineffective in a situation like this. An unwilling and fearful witness is no help. And we wouldn't seek a contempt citation.

"Let me explain," I said. "Please."

A short pause, then the door was unlatched and opened.

Rosario Ramirez was middle aged, with dark brown hair streaked with silver. She wore a cream-colored blouse with embroidery along the neckline, paired with blue cotton pants and white canvas sneakers. All I knew about her was that she was a widow.

"Thank you," I said.

"What do you want to show me?"

I took out my phone and brought up the photo of our client, Armando Molina.

"Is this the man you saw who did the shooting?" I said.

She looked at it, then quickly at me. "How do you know what I saw?"

"You deserve an answer, Mrs. Ramirez. Would you mind if we sat and I told you about it?"

She hesitated, then opened the door wider for me.

The living room had a hardwood floor with a large Aztec-design rug in the middle. The once vibrant reds and yellows were faded now. On one wall was a framed picture of the Virgin Mary. Below that, on a small wood table, were half a dozen votive candles in glass holders.

Mrs. Ramirez gestured to the sofa. I sat. She took the chair near the icon on the wall.

"I investigate for the defense in this matter," I said. "My job is to talk to people and find out what I can. The prosecutor and the police do the same thing. Sometimes we find different people. And I found someone who was willing to talk and said she believed you were an eyewitness to the shooting. Her name is Blanca Navarro."

Mrs. Ramirez nodded. "She is a neighbor of my cousin. I was visiting."

"And you saw the shooting?"

"How did you find me? Did she tell you where I live?"

"Only that you had gone back to Los Banos. That you didn't want to be involved."

"How did you find my house?"

"I know this sounds terrible," I said. "But I hope you understand we have an obligation to find any lead that we can. These days the computer can help us locate people."

"I do not like that," she said.

"I don't, either. We did get a phone number and I did try calling a couple of times but got no answer."

She nodded.

"I thought if I came here, I could explain," I said.

She closed her eyes, shook her head slowly. I looked at the picture behind her and heard myself say, "The Blessed Virgin."

She opened her eyes.

"Nuestra Señora de Guadalupe," she said.

"Our Lady of Guadalupe," I said.

"You speak Spanish?"

"Only in fits and starts," I said.

"Your name is Mike?"

"Yes."

"And I will not have to talk in court?"

"If you don't wish to be called, we won't call you."

She put her hands together, in the form of prayer, and rested her chin on them.

"Show me the picture again," she said.

I showed her.

"That is not the man," she said, then quickly added, "Is he of a gang?"

"He used to be," I said. "But he left the life and has been working a steady job."

"Why is he the one they think?"

"According to Armondo, he was set up by a rival gang. There are three who will swear he was the shooter. Can you be sure he was not?"

"The one I saw in the car, the one with the gun, that was not him."

"Can you describe the man you saw?"

"His face was not like that. It was, how can I say, pointed. This face is more round, like someone who is big."

"Big?"

"You know, *gordo*."

"Armando is that, as he'll readily admit."

She said, "I am sorry you had to come all this way."

"That's alright," I said. "I like to drive anyway. And I like to get out of the city from time to time."

When she didn't say anything, I said, "Would you at least be willing to sign a statement about what you've told me?"

Concern etched her face. She seemed like she wanted to help, but that desire was held back by her fear. For a moment I thought she might cry.

"Never mind," I said. "Is there anything else you feel comfortable telling me?"

She thought about it, then shook her head.

I stood. I gave her one of Ira's cards. "Thank you for talking to me. I know this is hard. If anything else occurs to you, please call this number. You can be sure that anything you say to us will remain confidential."

She stood and said, "I will say a prayer. I will say a prayer and think very hard about what you have said."

I put out my hand and we shook. "That's all anyone can ask, Mrs. Ramirez."

It was getting dark and I needed a place to zonk. There was a Motel 6 just off the freeway. I got a room, then went hunting for food. I had my pick of Wendy's, Jack in the Box, and Del Taco. I chose Jack's sumptuous menu and brought it back to my hovel. I munched while watching the news out of San Francisco, where the mayor was making some sort of pronouncement sure to leave the city worse off than it now was.

But that's California for you.

I searched around and found a channel showing Have Gun, Will Travel, a show my dad loved. Dr. Rexford Chamberlain, PhD., Professor of Philosophy and Aquinas scholar, thought Paladin the ideal hero because he used his mind more than his gun.

In this episode, Paladin reluctantly had to shoot a man who would not back down. Paladin tried to reason with him, but reason finds no purchase in the minds of outlaws with guns. Paladin had to dispatch the bad guy to Boot Hill.

Sufficiently satisfied that justice had been served, I called Sophie to say good night.

"Good night, sweet prince," Sophie said.

"You're quoting Hamlet," I said. "But he's dead at that point."

"Would you prefer Prince Charming?"

"If the shoe fits," I said.

"That shoe might be a little too tight on you," Sophie said. "You're more of a flip flop guy."

"Loose and easy?"

"With the occasional slip up."

"As long as you're there to catch me," I said.

"I'll be there," she said.

"I'll be home tomorrow."

"Don't drive slow."


Next morning I showered and shaved and checked out. I grabbed a breakfast burrito and coffee from Del Taco, pledging to eat only avocados and cruciferous greens—and Sophie's chile rellenos—when I got home.

Home. And she'd be there. Who would have thought it?

Not you, Romeo. Too much darkness in your past, danger in your presence, uncertainty in your future. A trifecta of existential dread.

Then one day you walk into a bookstore and see her. She takes your breath away and a little spark, like stone against flint, lights up the night inside you, and for a brief flash you wonder if it might be possible to be with her.

Then reality throws water on the flame. You know it would be dangerous for any woman to be with you because death seems always to be lurking around corners, in the shadows, ready to pounce.

But Sophie kept being there, and wanting to stay, and finally told me she doesn't care about doubts or fears, she only wants to be with me, and I knew I wanted to be with her, that I couldn't imagine being with any other.

So we were married. Ira officiated in front of witnesses— my beach friends, C Dog and Dr. Artra Murray—and Sophie's widower father. He gripped my hand after and, with tears in his eyes said, "Take care of her."

I pledged that I would. I would have signed that pledge in blood if he'd asked me to.

I'd gone about ten miles when I got a call. It was Maria.

"He came here last night," she said. "Dante! He told me to tell him what I knew about you. I told him nothing, to go away, but he came into the house. Papito stood up from his chair and yelled at him to leave. Dante pushed him down."

"You need to call the police," I said.

"It won't help."

"Call anyway. Get it on the record."

"I thought you would want to know."

"I do. I'm on my way down. See you in about an hour."

.   .   .

Maria was waiting for me outside the house.

"I made my father get in bed," she said. "He is very angry."

"Did you call the police?" I said.

She nodded.

"Did they send anybody?"

"No. They took down information."

I said, "I'm going to try to find out what's going on."

"What can you do?"

"I can talk to people," I said.

"Don't you have to go home?"

"I'm not on a schedule."

"But who will you talk to?" Maria said.

"Let's start with the fight," I said. "There were people in the diner who saw it."

She thought a moment. "The only one I know is Isidro Gallegos. He was sitting at the counter. He asked me if I was all right."

"He saw the fight?"

"Yes."

"Do you know how I can contact him?"

"He works at Treasure Almond Farm."

"Where's that?"

"I can take you there."

"Good," I said. "I'll drive."


The farm was five miles away. It had a dirt road that ran between two rows of almond trees. Scattered workers were among them.

We pulled up to an adobe-style building and got out. Inside was a little store with various displays of packaged almonds.

Behind the counter was a guy in his twenties. He looked like the lead in a soap opera, with a smile to prove it.

"Maria!" he said.

"Hello Juan," she said. "Is Isidro around?"

Juan came out from behind the counter, looking at me the whole way.

"This is my friend, Mike," she said.

We shook hands.

"Is he the one?" Juan said. "Isidro told me about the fight."

"He's the one," Maria said.

"You are most welcome here," Juan said. "Wish I could have seen it."

"Not much to see," I said.

"Oh, no," Juan said. "*Very* much."

"We'd like to ask Isidro about it," Maria said.

"He's out in the rows. Come."

Juan took us through the back, past processing equipment and stacks of boxes. We went outside through double doors. He pointed. "Most likely there," he said.

"Thanks, Juan," Maria said.

"Be sure to come back in," Juan said. "I want to give you samples."

As we walked down the path, I said, "Nice fellow."

"He's the son of the owner," Maria said. "We've known each other a long time."

We came to a spot where there was an empty golf cart. It had a clipboard on the seat.

A voice said, "Hola, Maria!"

A man came toward us. He wore jeans and a work shirt with the sleeves rolled up.

"Hello, Isidro," Maria said.

He smiled at me and stuck out his hand. I shook it.

"I am glad to see you again," he said. "You did a good thing."

"I'm trying to find out what that fight was all about," I said. "Do you have any idea?"

"That cabrón, no good."

"Any idea who the kid was?" I said.

He shook his head. It looked like all I was going to get here was a pack of almonds.

But then he said, "On the car ... how you say, the back." He made a stretch motion with his hands.

"A bumper sticker?" Maria said.

"Sí, the college."

"Drake College," Maria said. "Not too far away."

"That's a place to start," I said.

"You listen," Isidro said. "Be careful of cabrón. He killed a man."

"Why is he walking around?" I said.

Maria said, "Police said it was self defense."

"You don't sound convinced," I said.

"I'm not," Maria said.

Isidro put his hand on my shoulder. "Careful, yes?"

"Careful, yes," I said.


We went back in the store and Juan gave us a bag full of almond samples. He told us to come back any time.

I drove Maria back to her place. We talked in the car.

"Are you going to the college?" she said.

"Yes," I said.

"Do you want me to go with you?"

"No," I said. "Look after your pa."

"Please," she said. "What Isidro said. Be careful."

"And what about you? This punk may come back to the diner. Or your house."

"My father took out his gun," she said.

I smiled. "Good."

D rake College was a mile west of the 5. As I turned off the freeway I saw a knot of young people, probably students, holding a banner so the passing cars could see it. The banner said NO MORE FACTORY FARMS!

I couldn't help wondering if one or more of these whelps was the cow killer. What a student activity. Used to be frat boys would exercise their adrenal glands by toilet-papering a sorority house. Environmental studies majors would hold drum circles and chant pagan odes to Gaia and Demeter. The poli-sci naifs got their jollies shouting down speakers who dared to offer ideas that might throw a wrench into their indoctrinated brains. At least death wasn't on the table. Now it was.

All hail higher education.

Drake looked like an old high school with a recent facelift. I parked in an outside lot. I walked past a classroom building and into a lunch area. About a dozen students were around, some walking, some sitting, some eating. Every one of them was looking at a phone. Hard to blame them. Growing up drenched in digital, they know not the pleasure of uninterrupted conversation, or the restorative power of unplugged loafing.

At one table were two women and one man, if one can make such judgments these days. I wanted to say, "Hey, kids, have you ever had the pleasure of reading Moby-Dick?"

Not wishing to shock them, I settled for, "Greetings."

Three sets of eyes glanced at me. Two sets went back to their phones. One of the women, with a pixie haircut, stayed with me and said, "What's up?"

"I'm looking for a fellow student," I said.

"Who?" she said.

"I don't know his name. He's about five ten or so, drives a red Toyota."

Pixie frowned in a knowing way. "What do you want him for?"

"I want to know how he's doing," I said. "I helped him out of a bad situation."

The male of the species, still looking at his phone, said, "What situation?"

"Somebody was pounding his face," I said.

That brought all eyes to me again.

The girl who hadn't been heard from yet said, "I think I know who it might be."

"Don't say anything," the boy said. "We don't know who this guy is."

I said, "I'm from L.A., but don't hold that against me. I was just passing through and made a stop and was able to help one of your students who was getting beat down, okay?"

This seemed to confuse the lad. He was being asked to make a moral decision, and that was apparently beyond his skill set.

Girl 2 said, "He probably brought it on himself."

"What's that mean?" I said.

"He's a douche," she said.

"Shut up," the guy said.

"You shut up," Girl 2 said.

"This guy have a name?" I said.

Now Girl 2 looked conflicted and didn't say anything.

At which point a security guard stepped into the scene and said, "Can I help you?"

He was a young one, student age. His uniform was baggy, his sandy hair tousled like Huckleberry Finn.

"I'm looking for a student who got hurt in a fight yesterday," I said. "I gave him some help and wanted to check on him."

"You need a visitor badge," Security said.

"I'd sure appreciate it if you got me one."

He shook his head. "Have to check in at the office. This way." He started to walk off with his arm out for me to follow.

"I'll be right with you," I said.

"Uh-uh," he said. "Now."

To the student trio I said, "I'll be right back."

I joined Security, who said as we walked, "It's the rules."

"Rules are good," I said. "Until they're not."

"What?"

"A good rule can become unjust, depending on the context."

He frowned and didn't say anything.

"Maybe you know the student I'm trying to contact," I said. "He drives a red Toyota and got in a fight yesterday with a guy named Dante. Heard anything about that?"

Security thought a moment, shook his head. We were at the admin building and he opened the door for me and we went in.

A young woman in a Drake sweatshirt sat at the front desk, keyboarding in front of a monitor. She looked up as we approached.

"He needs a visitor badge," Security said.

The woman smiled. "All right. And what is the nature of your visit?"

"I'd like to talk to a student I helped out of some trouble yesterday," I said.

"Trouble?"

"In the nature of a fight," I said. "He was getting pounded pretty bad and I stopped it. I just want to know how he's doing."

"The student's name?"

"I don't know," I said.

"I'm afraid we need the name," she said. "We would have to notify the student first to see if he wants to see you."

"There's a group of students I just talked to," I said. "They seem to know who he is."

"You were on campus?"

"He just walked on," Security said.

"You just walked on?" the woman said.

"I learn by going where I have to go," I said.

They both looked at me.

"It's from a poem," I said. "I went to college, too."

"Would you mind waiting a moment?" the woman said.

"My feet are planted firmly on the earth," I said.

The woman frowned and picked up a handset.

"What are you about, man?" Security said.

"Excuse me?" I said.

"What's your deal?"

"Do I have to have a deal?" I said.

"Why do you talk like that?" he said.

"Like what?" I said.

"Poems, and feet on the earth and stuff."

"To spice up conversations," I said.

"Why?"

"Don't you think conversations these days need some spice?" I said. "Would you have life be plain eggs? Wouldn't you like an omelet with ham, cheese, cilantro and Tapatio?"

"To tell you the truth, man, you make me kind of nervous."

"Like maybe I have a screw loose?"

"Well…"

"Let me assure you, my good fellow, that I attempt to keep all my screws in place, and tightened. I'm not here to cause trouble or make people nervous. I am legitimately trying to help out a guy who was in some trouble."

He paused. "All right."

"Can we shake on it?"

I put out my hand and, after a moment, he took it.

Which is when severe looking woman with tortoise-shell glasses came into the reception area through a side door.

"Can I help you?" she said in a manner that suggested she didn't want to help at all.

"I'm trying to get in touch with one of your students," I said.

"Why is that?"

"I'm from Los Angeles. I work for a lawyer. I was eating at Gussie's Diner yesterday and saw a fight break out. This student was involved and took the worst of it. I stopped the fight and helped him get patched up, but he drove off. I wanted to see how he was doing."

"The student's name?"

"He didn't give us his name."

"Us?"

"A waitress at the diner helped him out, too."

"How do you know he is a student here?"

"He had a Drake bumper sticker on his car."

"Lots of people do," she said. "Some are alumni, some are parents."

"If I could just ask around," I said. "Some students in the lunch area seemed to know who it might be."

"Your name?"

"Mike Romeo."

She adjusted her glasses. "I'm sorry, Mr. Romeo, but we can't allow just anyone on campus, the way things are."

"What things?" I said.

She gave the other two a look, then said, "Would you mind stepping into my office?"

"I'd be delighted," I said.

. . .

S he led me to the door she'd come through. There was a hallway and a couple of cubicles. I followed her into a small office. She closed the door.

She said, "Surely you know about violence on campuses, even shootings."

How well I did know. My parents, professors both, were gunned down at Yale when I was a student there.

"I do," I said.

"We have to be vigilant," she said. "Things have been tense lately."

"The factory farms thing?"

"You're aware of that?"

"Only what I've observed," I said. "It's hard to miss the big banner by the freeway."

"Have a seat, Mr. Romeo."

I took one of the chairs in front of her desk. The nameplate on the desk read *Gretchen Forrester, Dean of Students.*

She sat behind the desk. "We have a responsibility to protect our students."

"I understand that," I said. I took out one of Ira's lawyer cards and handed it to her. "This is the lawyer. You can check him out."

She gave the card a quick scan, then set it aside. "We still need a name."

"I was close to getting it," I said. "If I could talk to those students out in the lunch area."

"I'm sorry, Mr. Romeo."

"You really are careful," I said. "I'll give you another name. Dante."

"Dante? The poet?"

"Dante Hooker, local thug."

She paused before shaking her head. I read something in that pause. I suspected she knew.

"I guess I'll have to keep on digging," I said.

"Please, not here," Gretchen Forrester said.

"If you don't mind," I said, "I'd like to hear what the general vibe is around here concerning the cattle industry."

"Are you really interested?" she said.

"I'm always open to learning new things," I said.

She leaned back in her chair. She was a teacher now.

"Do you realize," she said, her voice clipped and precise, "there are twenty billion head of livestock on this planet? That's more than triple the number of people. They're taking up so much space, consuming so much resource. It's staggering."

I nodded, inviting her to continue.

"Americans spend $110 billion a year on fast food." She paused, letting the number hang in the air. "That's more than they spend on higher education. More than movies, books, magazines, newspapers, videos, and recorded music combined."

"Big Macs are winning the culture war," I said.

"It's not funny," she said. "The 4.8 pounds of grain fed to cattle to produce just one pound of beef, that's a colossal waste of resources. All while millions of people go hungry or suffer from malnutrition. Explain to me how that makes sense."

"You're saying the system's broken."

"Broken doesn't even begin to cover it," she said. "It's destructive. Energy intensive factory farms in the U.S. produce 1.4 billion tons of animal waste. That waste pollutes American waterways more than all other industrial sources combined. And let's not even start on soil erosion, billions of acres of once productive farmland lost. Rainforests destroyed for grazing. All for what?"

"Steak and eggs?" I said.

She sighed. "Meat production is one of the biggest contributors to climate change. Methane's a planet warming gas, and cows are the single largest agricultural source. They produce nearly ten percent of all greenhouse gas emissions via anterior enteric fermentation."

"Cow farts?" I said.

"It's serious. And if we keep going down this path, we're taking the planet with us."

"Maybe the science is wrong on this one," I said.

"Excuse me?"

"If we've learned anything the past six years, it's that results can be manipulated, wouldn't you agree?"

She dug in. "No, I would not. Otherwise what is expertise for?"

"Even experts disagree."

"Outliers, perhaps."

"But what if the inliers are liars? It's been known to happen."

She folded her hands on the desk. "Mr. Romeo, you asked me the way I see it, and I've told you. If you want to debate someone, perhaps I can introduce you to one of our professors."

"I'm a little pressed for time. How about this? If you happen to find out who the student is, his face will have bruises, would you tell him about me? And call the number on the card?"

"All right," she said, in a tone that indicated, "*Probably not.*"


I went back to my car, feeling Security's eyes on my back. I gave him a wave as I got in. He waved back.

I got in and called Ira.

"You're not back yet," Ira said.

"Well observed," I said. "I may be delayed."

"What's going on?"

"You remember that altercation I told you about?"

"You think I'd forget?"

"There's more to it," I said.

"I'm not surprised."

"And I need another couple of days to figure it out."

"When are you going to tell me what it is?" Ira said.

"I'll type up a report and send it to you, how's that?"

"When?"

"Tonight. I'll be checking into a motel."

"And what about our witness?"

"I'll put that in the report," I said. "The short answer is she is positive the shooter is not Armando."

"Excellent!"

"But she doesn't want to testify," I said. "She's afraid of the gangs."

"Is she firm on that?"

"Absolutely," I said. "She did say she would pray about it."

"Well, that's something."

"If she could be persuaded to make a sworn statement, can we use it?"

"We can make a motion, based on her fear. But in a murder case, courts are loathe to allow that. The Sixth Amendment is one solid cornerstone."

"Doggone Bill of Rights," I said.

"Genius Bill of Rights," Ira said.

"Applies to the government," I said.

"Meaning?"

"Just that I'm a citizen," I said. "Every now and then I may have to ignore the Fourth Amendment."

"Michael, I am an officer of the court. I cannot sanction—"

"You don't have to sanction," I said.

"Meaning?"

"I just won't tell you."

"Michael!"

"I love you too, Ira."

A fter that I called Sophie.
"Hey, guess what?" I said.
"You won the lottery?" she said.
"I did," I said. "First prize, you."
"You're sweet."
"In other news, I'll be delayed coming home."
"What? Why?"
"That fight I told you about?"
"Yes?"
"It was outside a diner," I said. "The guy I put down was beating up on a kid half his size. He apparently has a rep up here. A waitress in the diner helped me look after the kid, who drove off like a scared rabbit. The waitress warned me about the punk. She had me follow her to her house where she lives with her dad, an Army vet who's on oxygen. After I left to go to Los Banos, this punk, whose name is Dante Hooker, paid a visit to the house and threatened them. He wanted to know all about me. He assaulted the dad. I figure that was my fault, and I owe them."

"What, exactly, do you owe?" Sophie said.

"Protection, maybe. And answers. I want to find out why this Dante was beating up this kid, who's apparently a student at a little college up here. I'm trying to find him."

"Does Ira know about this?"

"I'm going to send him a report. Which I get to write up in some motel room."

"Another motel?"

"My glamorous life on the road."

"I miss you," she said.

"That's a coincidence," I said. "I miss you, too."

"Let's remedy that. I have a little flex time right now. I'll come to you."

"You want to drive up here?" I said.

"Will I be in your way?"

"I certainly hope so," I said.

"Hurry up and find that motel," she said.

I looked up the address for the Central Valley Dispatch. It was located at the end of a strip mall, between a nail salon and a place called Burrito Bueno. I went through the glass door. Inside were desks and computers. One of them was occupied by a woman with glasses attached to a neck chain. She looked up from her monitor and said, "Hello."

"Hi there," I said. "My name's Mike Romeo. I'm from L.A."

"Good place to be from," she said with a smile. "How do you stand it?"

"I live at the beach," I said.

"That helps," she said. "What can I do for you?"

"I was wondering if Jamie Anderson is around."

"Not today," she said. "He's probably working at home."

"Is there a way I can get in touch with him?"

"May I ask what this is in regard to?"

"I'd be disappointed if you didn't," I said.

She smiled. "What can I tell him?"

"I'm just passing through, but along the way I made a couple of contacts here. I read his story about the poisoning of the cows. I wanted to ask him about that."

"May I ask why?"

"I'm gathering information. I work for a lawyer in Los Angeles as an investigator. I want to know more about the controversies up here. I was just out at Drake College and saw a protest going on near the freeway."

"Oh, yes," she said. "Well, you've come to the right place. Mr. Peale is all over this."

"Mr. Peale?"

"Our publisher and editor-in-chief."

"Would he happen to be around?" I said.

A man's voice said, "He would be." He was dressed in rumpled slacks and an Oxford shirt that needed ironing. The sleeves were rolled up. The slacks were held by red suspenders. He was probably sixty years old, but moved with a certain grace. He might have played high school or college football. His gray hair was cut in military style and he smiled with a friendly inquisitiveness.

"I'm Bill Peale," he said.

"Mike Romeo."

We shook hands. "You have business with us? Or maybe a scoop?"

"Nothing as exciting as that." I gave him the same information I gave to the woman.

"Why don't we step into my office?" he said.


Sardines would have felt right at home in his cramped office. Every bit of wall was covered with framed photos, pinned notes, and paint the color of cinnamon oatmeal. A squatty desk sat in the middle, covered with papers, its corners scarred like the eyes of an old boxer. There was a classic manual typewriter on one side and a closed laptop on the other. A not unpleasant smell of pipe tobacco hung in the air.

Peale motioned to a folding chair. "Have a seat," he said, then parked himself in a wooden swivel chair that creaked like it was 1959.

He winked. "Here's where I do my genius work."

"Perfect environment for it," I said.

"I like being packed in," he said. "Focuses the mind. So you're interested in the goings on up here?"

"Just by accident," I said. "I read the story of the poisoned cows. What's the beef?"

He smiled. "I've heard that one before."

"I tend to recycle witticisms," I said.

"There's a big movement against meat, as you probably know."

"Ethical treatment of animals," I said.

"Not just that. There's the heady brew of hate."

I nodded. "A dopamine rush."

"That's right," he said. "Kids want meaning, a cause, want to be part of a group. A group that offers hate is dispensing a drug. On college campuses it's as pervasive as fentanyl."

"Speaking of which, I was out at Drake College. I'm trying to locate a student there I had the opportunity to help out of a bad situation."

"Bad situation?"

I told him about my fight with Dante.

"Yeah, Dante," Bill Peale said. "He's known around here. Claims to be private security to protect student protesters."

"Who pays him?" I said.

"We haven't been able to find that out."

"Any idea who the kid he beat up might be?"

"You say he goes to Drake?"

"A couple of students seemed to know who I was talking about. They didn't have good things to say about him, but wouldn't give up his name."

"I can do some research," Peale said. "Might be a good lead for a story."

"Maybe we can work together," I said.

"I think I'd like that." He paused. "You mind telling me what the tattoo on your arm says? It looks like Latin."

"It is," I said. "Truth conquers all things."

"Nice," he said. "Truth is why I went into the news game."

"Would that more journalists were in the game for that."

"You speak truly," he said with a grin. "You'd make a great columnist. How would you like a byline?"

"I'm flattered you asked," I said. "But I do my talking in other ways."

"Let's at least keep in touch," he said.

"Absolutely," I said. "Would you mind if I talked to Jamie Anderson?"

"Not at all. Good kid. Great potential. Let's exchange numbers and I'll have him get in touch with you."

We made the exchange. Peale stood and we shook hands.

"Just watch your back out there," Peale said. "There are things going on beneath the surface."

"Which is why we need good old-fashioned newspaper editors."

"Ain't *that* the truth?" he said, and laughed. It was a laugh of defiance.


I did some searching for a motel. I was tired of the sameness of the chains. A name that popped up was The Somber Sloth. I had to see what it looked like.

At least it looked clean. I parked and approached the office. Two brick-lined flower beds displayed abundant blooms, always a draw for me.

No one was in the office. Behind a small counter was a computer and monitor. Off to the side a table with an instant coffee setup—a water kettle, a jar of instant labeled "One of the Perks," a cup with plastic stirrers and a bowl of sugar packets. A Felix the Cat wall clock ticked, with Felix's eyes going back and forth.

A woman came out of the back. She was small and wore

rubber cleaning gloves. She took them off and said, "May I help you?"

"I'd like a room," I said.

"Of course. Will you be staying long?"

"A day or two," I said.

She started tapping the computer.

"I like your marguerite daisies," I said.

"My what?"

"Your flowers."

"Aren't they sunflowers?"

"They're argyranthemum frutescens," I said. "Especially hardy for the summer months."

"How do you know about that?" she said.

"It's a hobby of mine."

"That's funny," she said.

"What is?"

"You don't look like somebody who'd be into flowers."

"I've been told that."

"You here on business?" she said.

"A little," I said.

She finished her tapping, I paid her, she gave me a key card.

"Right up the outside stairs," she said. "My name is Elena. Let me know if you need anything. Enjoy your stay."


I n the room I called Sophie and gave her the address.

"Look for the argyranthemum frutescens," I said.

"Let me guess. Flowers."

"Yellow daisies," I said. "You better pack me some clothes, too."

"I'll see you tomorrow," she said.

I opened my laptop and typed a report on the Los Banos

witness interview and sent it to Ira. Then took a few minutes to scan the news.

A group of failed politicians and less than influential influencers had formed a new action group, dedicated to "saving the soul of America." It sounded oddly familiar. Ah yes, history. This was the same verbiage employed by southern Democrats after the Civil War when they formed the Ku Klux Klan. Apparently history was a subject missed by this lot in school.

Then there was a case up in San Francisco, of a Navy veteran who was riding on Bay Area Rapid Transit when a crackhead threatened an old woman and grabbed a handful of her dress. While other passengers trained their phones on the crime-in-progress, the vet jumped up and gave the crackhead a punch in the face. The crackhead fell backwards and bumped his head, which itself cracked. And killed him. The vet was charged with manslaughter. The judge all but instructed the jury to bring in a verdict of guilty. But in a stunning turn of events, the jury employed what lawyers call jury nullification. That means a jury can bring back any verdict it wants, despite what a judge says, if they feel an injustice is being done. The Navy vet was found not guilty. Heads were exploding all over the City by the Bay and on news sites no one reads anymore.

The two stories went together in my head. What was saving the soul of America wasn't a group of disgruntled eggheads, but men like this Navy vet who stepped up to do what men used to do by instinct—protect women in physical danger. For years that instinct has been rubbed out of boys and young men. Here was a sign that maybe, just maybe, it was coming back.

I spread myself out on the bed, and imagined having Sophie beside me. It was a wonderfully strange feeling. Mike Romeo was married. That's something I never thought would happen.

Yet it had. And I knew I was changed, but in ways I couldn't fully comprehend. I closed my eyes. A vision of Sophie on our wedding day floated into my mind. She was in a white dress and had a blue orchid tucked behind her ear. Her hazel eyes gleamed. She was about to say "I will" when my phone buzzed.

It was Jamie Anderson. "Mr. Peale said you wanted to talk to me."

"I would," I said. "Can we meet?"

"Can you tell me why?"

"It has to do with a guy, a student at Drake, who I helped out in a fight. I'm trying to find him."

"Again, why?"

"You really are an intrepid reporter, aren't you."

"I try."

"Is there a problem?" I said.

"I have to be careful," he said.

"I understand that. My whole life is based on being careful."

Pause. "Okay. There's a little park at the corner of Willard and Rust. Do you know where that is?"

"I can find it."

"Say half an hour?"

"Works for me."

"How will I know you?" he said.

"I'll be wearing a white carnation and carrying a copy of The Wall Street Journal."

"Seriously?"

"That's the way it was done it the movies," I said. "Actually, I'm six-four and will be wearing a Hawaiian shirt."

"That should do it," he said.

.   .   .

D aylight was fading when I got to the park. It was mostly grass, some dirt, and had a kids' play area in one corner. A woman with a stroller watched a boy of five or six climbing up a little rock wall that led to a slide. The boy whooped as he came down the slide, arms in the air.

A guy sat on a bench, looking at his phone. On the slender side, he had dark hair, glasses, and wore a sport coat with an open-collared white shirt. He looked up as I walked over.

"Jamie?" I said.

"Mr. Romeo?" he said.

"How could you tell?"

He smiled. "You're exactly as you described."

"I try to be precise." I sat on the bench and shook his hand. "Thanks for meeting me."

"Mr. Peale vouched for you," he said. "You're interested in finding a Drake student?"

"Yes." I told him about the fight at Gussie's.

"I wish I could have seen that," Jamie said. "Dante Hooker has quite the rep."

"Bluster and beef," I said.

"How's that?"

"Mouth and muscle. He depends on those two things. He's not too skilled as a fighter."

"He's dangerous, though," Jamie said. "You've made an enemy."

"There's a long list," I said.

"What is it exactly that you do, Mr. Romeo?"

"Call me Mike. I'm an investigator for a lawyer in L.A. That sometimes runs into trouble."

"You look like you can handle yourself."

"I did some cage fighting," I said. "Not much to put on a resumé, though."

"And you're interested in investigating the beef industry up here?"

"If it helps me understand what happened at Gussie's."

Jamie sat back, crossed his legs. "There's all sorts of things happening. The cow poisonings is one of those things."

"You have a theory?" I said.

"A theory, but no proof," he said.

"Lay it on me."

"This is all confidential, right?"

"Right."

"I'm only talking to you because Mr. Peale said it's okay."

"I have a proven record of keeping my lip zipped," I said.

He nodded. "Okay. Have you heard of Caleb Crane?"

"A tech billionaire, right?"

"Right. Founded the social media platform, PZZAZA. It's supposedly revolutionizing the way people connect and share information. Advanced AI driving content recommends. And integrates it with virtual reality."

"Must sell a lot of wrap-around headsets."

"Also massive advertising revenue," Jaimie said. "PZZAZA for putting more pizzaz in interactivity, I guess. He also has a company that produces an AI-driven personal assistant for businesses and individuals. It's called Maxtail, named for his childhood dog, Max, with the idea that the tail will wag the dog now. In other words, his company will reshape the world of tech and after that, the world itself."

"I like modest goals," I said.

"That's not all," Jamie said. "He's a rabid environmentalist. He's bought up huge swaths of land. He wants to end beef production, or at least make it too expensive to operate."

"You think he's gunning for Rendell Ranch?"

"That's my theory," Jamie said. "Have you met Travis Rendell?"

"No."

"You should. He's a legend. They're having an annual mover and shaker dinner there tomorrow. I'm tight with them. I can get you in."

"For dinner?"

"Best steak you'll ever eat," Jamie said.

"I'm there. Can I bring a guest?"

"Guest?"

"My wife."

"Your wife is with you?"

"She will be. Her name's Sophie."

"Absolutely," Jamie said. "And I'll try to find out who that Drake student is."

"I'd appreciate that," I said.

We left it there. Jamie shook my hand and walked off into the twilight. I stayed. It was quiet. The woman with the stroller and the boy were gone. I sat there wondering how far this thing was going to go. It really wasn't any of my business. But when a thug starts threatening women and old men, the old fire starts to flame.

I n the morning I went to Gussie's for breakfast. Maria wasn't there. The waitress named Ruth was serving. I sat at the counter. Ruth was talking to a man at the other end. When she saw me she smiled and came over.

"Nice to see you again," she said. "Coffee?"

"Please."

She turned to the two coffee carafes behind her, poured a cup, and set it in front of me.

"Maria not here today?" I said.

"She has to take her dad to Fresno for a doctor appointment."

"How's he doing?" I said.

"Holding on," Ruth said. "He's tough. I just love him.

Need a few minutes?"

"Not at all," I said. "I'll have eggs over medium, bacon, hash browns, and sourdough toast."

"You got it," she said.

A stack of actual newspapers sat at the end of the counter. I grabbed one. It was The Central Valley Dispatch.

The lead story was about football. The Central High Lions had "roared back" to defeat the heavily favored Creekside Chargers in a "nail-biting" 27-24 victory. The Lions quarterback, a kid named Ethan Morales, sparked the comeback win. With twelve seconds left, Morales scrambled on fourth-and-goal and whipped a bullet to his tailback in the end zone.

It was nice to read some good news for a change.

Inside the paper were items about local events—a farmer's market, a church picnic, and a school board meeting that was "contentious" because of a budget shortfall. They were discussing cutbacks to after-school programs at Central High, including Marching Band, which did not sit well with several parents in attendance. That made me happy. At least, for a change, they weren't fighting bathroom battles, boys in girls' locker rooms, or porn in the library.

There was a Letters to the Editor page, and an opinion piece written by Bill Peale. I wondered if our little talk had inspired it.

In an era where news spreads faster than ever—often with little regard for accuracy—it's worth pausing to reflect on the role of trusted, local journalism. Here at The Central Valley Dispatch, we believe that the cornerstone of a strong community is reliable information, delivered with integrity and transparency.

National headlines are dominated by sensationalism, clickbait, and an alarming lack of accountability. Social media amplifies the noise, often blurring the line between fact and opinion. But what about the stories that truly matter? The ones that connect us as neighbors—like last night's thrilling Lions victory—or keep us informed about local issues, from agriculture to education?

In a world where trust in media feels mighty fragile, let's not lose sight of what matters: truth, fairness, and the shared stories that make this valley home.

I read the whole paper as I ate my breakfast. Ruth re-filled my coffee cup a couple of times. The place got crowded. I noticed a guy in a blue uniform and badge sitting in a booth by the window.

A question popped into my head. I went over to him.

"Morning," I said.

He looked up from his pancakes. He made not smiling look easy.

"Mind if I ask you a question?" I said.

"I'm eating breakfast," he said. "Not on duty."

"That's okay," I said. "I'm not either."

I sat opposite him.

"Hey, I didn't ask you to sit down," he said.

"I'm harmless," I said.

"Who are you?"

"My name's Mike. I'm from out of town."

He looked at my shirt. "I never would have guessed."

"I wanted to know if you're familiar with a guy named Dante."

His jaw twitched. "Why?"

"I have a feeling your department knows who he is."

"I don't know who you are," he said. "And I don't have to answer your questions."

"True enough," I said. "But I assume you have the interests of the local citizens at heart, like a good policeman should. I just want to know what you'd do if you found out Dante was making threats against people."

He put his fork down on his plate and wiped his mouth with a napkin. "Look, if you've got a complaint, go to the station and report it."

"Suppose I report it to you?"

"I'm going to finish my breakfast," he said. "I have nothing more to say to you."

"Far be it from me to get between a man and his food."

I slipped out of the booth.

"If you're here to make trouble, don't," the policeman said.

"Me? I'm a pussycat."

"Sure."

I went back to my meal. The hash browns were cold. I dotted them with Tapatio and finished them off. Ruth came over with the coffee pot.

"No more for me," I said.

"What was that all about?" she said.

"Just some unfriendly conversation," I said. "Know him?"

"Mark Jacobsen," she said. "He's a little sketchy."

"How?"

"There's just something about him. And I don't like serving him. He always undertips."

I finished my coffee and paid my check, which came to $19.47. I left a five for Ruth. I'm sketchy enough without undertipping.

On the way back to the motel I got a call from Sophie.

"I just passed Bakersfield," she said. "Should be there in a couple of hours."

"If you step on it, you could be here in an hour-and-a-half," I said.

"Stepping on it," she said.

. . .

I looked up a florist shop in town called Wild Petals. It was next to a laundromat. The smell of fresh sheets followed me in to the scent of floral arrangements. A young woman was behind the counter, a student type. She was arranging some carnations in a vase.

"Be with you in a moment," she said.

I went to the cooler and scoped out the offerings.

The woman came over. "Help you find something?"

"Nine red roses," I said.

"Nine?"

"Nine."

"Not a dozen?" she said.

"I'm married," I said. "A dozen red roses is when you're trying to win your true love. Nine is for the one you've pledged to spend your whole life with."

"Really?"

"In Chinese, nine is homonym for long lasting."

"Wow. I didn't know that."

"Nine long stems, please," I said.

"Absolutely." She opened the cooler and selected the roses. She took them to the counter and started to wrap them. She had a floral tattoo on her forearm.

"Nice ink," I said. "English lavender."

"That's right. My grandmother loved lavender."

"A lovely tribute," I said.

She looked at my arm. "What's yours?"

"Latin," I said. "My father loved Latin."

"What's it mean?"

"Truth conquers all things."

"Wow," she said. "Major slay."

"Meaning you approve?"

"We gotta believe in truth, right?"

"You have made my day," I said.

She smiled and finished the wrapping. "Anything else?"

"I need a vase," I said.

"Sure." She helped me pick one. I paid the bill.

"Your wife is a lucky woman," she said.

"I'm the lucky one," I said. "May I know your name?"

"Melody," she said.

"I'm Mike. Nice doing business with you."

"Come back anytime," she said.


B ack at the room I filled the vase with water and arranged the roses. I set them on the small table next to the bed. I opened my laptop and made notes in my chrono-log.

Then I did some research on Caleb Crane. Found a profile in the San Jose Mercury News. Crane was born into a wealthy family in Palo Alto. His father was a venture capitalist, his mother an environmental scientist. He attended an elite prep school and later enrolled at Stanford, where he earned a degree in computer science.

At Stanford he got involved with a grassroots environmental movement. He took part in a sit-in protest to stop deforestation for a commercial development. When private security tried to clear the area, a protestor threw a Molotov cocktail at a bulldozer, starting a fire that spread to nearby equipment and forested areas. One of the protestors was severely burned.

In the article, Crane was quoted as saying, "That showed me traditional activism is futile."

He went on to get an M.B.A. at Harvard. And then started founding the companies Jamie Anderson had told me about. Now he had the money to buy up large swaths of land.

"I am a friend to the Earth, and all who want to live on it in peace," he said.

And the road to hell is paved with good intentions, I thought.

That's when I heard a knock at the door. I threw it open.

Sophie jumped into my arms. She wrapped her legs around me and gave me what the simple word *kiss* hardly describes.

I slammed the door shut with my foot.

L ater, Sophie said, "Does this count as a honeymoon?"
We'd had plans to spend a week in Carmel by the Sea. But the criminal case of Armando Molina interrupted things.

"Let's call it a preview of a real honeymoon," I said. "A teaser."

"I can't wait for the feature," she said.

"You'll get it. The uncut version."

She laughed.

"Meanwhile," I said, "you should know what's going on."

I gave her the rundown on my doings.

She didn't say anything at first. I didn't care. The softness of her next to me could have gone on and on as far as I was concerned.

Finally, she said, "Can I ask you something?"

"That is, of course, your privilege," I said. "You can even tell me something."

"You mean it?"

I cleared my throat. "I think so."

She kissed my chest. "Only asking this time, because I'm still getting to know the onion that is you."

"I've been called many things," I said. "But an onion?"

"So many layers," she said. "But I happen to like onions."

"You can dice me any time, baby."

"Aw," she said. "So you're a sweet onion."

"Continue," I said.

"I was just wondering, how much is your staying up here

to help out a man and his daughter, and how much are you hoping to get another chance at this fellow Dante?"

Wow, I said to myself.

"Wow," I said to Sophie.

"Yes?"

"You really are getting to know me."

"It's a project," she said. "But I love my work."

"I admit it," I said. "I feel like I have unfinished business with him."

"Then I will offer one thought for your consideration. Consider that, in this case, discretion may be the better part of valor."

"Sophie Montag, are you trying to civilize me?"

"Now there's a project."

I said, "I pledge to you I shall uphold the virtues of Western Civilization. Such as goodness, truth"—I ran my finger over her lips—"and beauty."

"I like that," she whispered. "Tell me more."


Two hours later we were freshly showered and dressed for dinner. I had on my evening clothes—slacks and a clean Tommy Bahama shirt.

Sophie, who can make a laundry bag with arm holes look good, wore black slacks and a white, long-sleeve, button-down shirt.

"You're like a hot fudge sundae with whipped cream on top," I said.

Sophie said, "Talk like that is liable to sweep me off my feet."

"Then we better be going," I said.

. . .

The Rendell Ranch Resort was designed like one of the old Spanish haciendas that once spread across central and southern California. It had a wing of rooms and was dominated by a restaurant and market dedicated to all things beef.

In the lobby was a sign about the private party, directing us to a ballroom. We checked in at a table where a woman found our names on a list. She motioned to the open door behind her and said, "Enjoy yourselves."

The ballroom was decked out in American Cattle Drive motif. A set of huge steer horns hung on one wall next to a painting of a cowboy that was probably an original Frederic Remington. It was cocktail hour, and people were moving and shaking like the movers and shakers they had to be. Servers in cowboy dress served hors d'oeuvres and drinks.

One man dominated the room. You can tell those guys. He was big, like Matt Dillon, and wore a cowboy hat, a suit and a bolo tie with a turquoise slide. As he shook some hands he glanced our way, and immediately made a beeline over to us.

"You must be Mike Romeo," he said, extending his hand.

"You must be Travis Rendell," I said.

"Nice to meet ya." He turned to Sophie. "And you must be Sophie."

"I am," she said, and shook his hand.

"Jamie Anderson told me all about you," he said. "He told me to look for a big guy in a Hawaiian shirt. It appears you're the only one."

"I didn't bring my cowboy duds with me," I said.

"Never mind that," Rendell said. "I heard what you did at Gussie's. You've got dog in you, that's all that counts."

"You've got a nice place here," I said.

"Like my father before me," he said. "We Rendells, most of us anyway, think we're doing something so important…ah, listen to me prattle."

"Prattle on," I said. "I'd like to hear."

"Really?"

"Yep," I said with my best Western slang.

"And what about you, my dear?" Rendell said.

"I'd like to hear it too," Sophie said.

Travis Rendell smiled. "All right then! If I was to ask you what one thing built America, what would your answer be?"

"Big question," I said. "A number of things came together."

"Right you are. But there's one thing that helped us take off."

"Railroads?" Sophie said.

"Close! It's beef. The railroads carried the beef to Chicago. Beef was fed to the people. It built muscles, enabling men to do more of a man's work. It made strong women stronger, child bearing safer. It made smart women smarter and heck, women may be smarter than men to begin with."

"I like this man," Sophie said.

"Beef powers the brain," Rendell said. "The brain needs fats. All this low-fat nonsense of the past sixty years, what's the result? Ever wonder why dementia has spiked? Beef fat is what our bodies have been using for thousands of years. The problem is all these processed foods and trans fats and junk with processed oils. You know about cottonseed oil?"

"You cook with it," I said.

"Not if you're smart. It was designed to lubricate heavy machinery. At the turn of the century it started to be marketed as a healthy alternative to lard. You know what started to spike then? Heart disease. That was virtually unknown in the 1800s. Getting the picture?"

"Bring on the steak and butter," I said.

Rendell said, "What are you two drinkin'? Can I interest you in one of our local cabernets?"

"You can indeed," Sophie said.

"Make it two," I said.

Rendell motioned for a waiter and gave them our drink order.

"Let me introduce you to a few folks," Rendell said.

He looked around, but before he moved a woman smiled over to him. She was maybe forty-five with long blond hair, wearing a red evening dress over designer cowboy boots. She held a glass of red wine.

"Travis," she said, "who are your guests?"

"This is Mike Romeo and his wife, Sophie," Rendell said. "And this is Mary Lou Overstreet."

"Welcome," she said, and shook our hands.

Rendell said, "She keeps this place in line."

"Sustainable practices," Mary Lou Overstreet said.

"A good practice should be sustained," I said.

"Have they had a tour of the place?" Mary Lou said.

"Not yet," Travis Rendell said.

"I'll be sure to arrange it," Mary Lou said.

Somebody called to Rendell. "Excuse me for just a moment," he said, and walked over to a man and woman looking like they were ready for a square dance.

Mary Lou said, "What's your line of work, Mr. Romeo?"

"I work for a lawyer in L.A.," I said. "Sophie teaches middle school."

"Wonderful! And what brings you to our fair town?"

"A little business up north," I said.

"How do you know Travis?"

"We just met."

"He's impressive, isn't he?"

"He is," I said.

"He's a throwback to the Old West," Mary Lou said. "We don't have many like that left."

A waiter appeared with our drinks. I handed Sophie a glass and took the other for myself.

"Oh great," Mary Lou said. "Here comes Baldwin Fish. Keep your hand on your wallet."

A man who just walked out of an aftershave commercial came our way. His smiling teeth were the color of the snows of Kilimanjaro with the sun shining on it.

"Mary Lou," he said. "You are looking lovely tonight."

"I'll bet you say that to all your donors," Mary Lou said.

He gave me a side glance. "This your date?"

"Nope," Sophie said.

He turned to my wife. "Ah, then who do I have the pleasure of addressing?"

Mary Lou said, "This is Mike Romeo and his wife, Sophie."

"Very pleased to meet you," he said. He shook our hands. "New to the area?"

"Passing through," I said.

"Welcome!" Fish said. "We always like to have guests, and we treat them right."

"Baldwin is running for Congress," Mary Lou said.

"I never would have guessed," I said.

"You follow politics, Mr. Romeo?" Baldwin Fish said.

"A strife of interests masquerading as a contest of principles," I said.

Fish blinked a couple of times.

"Ambrose Bierce," I said. "The Devil's Dictionary."

"Rather cynical, don't you think?" Fish said.

"I run with Antisthenes," I said.

"I'm afraid I don't follow."

"Greek philosopher. Founder of the school of cynicism."

"Really?"

"He said the most useful piece of learning is to unlearn what is untrue."

Fish blinked again.

"Wow," Mary Lou said. "The first man who ever rendered you speechless, Baldwin."

Baldwin Fish broke out his thousand-watt smile. "You're a thinker, Mr. Romeo. Maybe we can chat again sometime."

"I do like a good chat," I said.

"Till we meet again." He gave Mary Lou Overstreet a peck on the cheek. Then he was off.

"He's a wily one," Mary Lou said.

"Perfect for California politics," I said.

We talked a little more, Mary Lou telling us about her job. With a pained expression she spoke of the cow poisonings and how they had a high-level private security firm looking into the matter. She talked a little about the protesters at Drake, but then changed the subject to more pleasant matters. She asked Sophie about her teaching. Then what it was like living at the beach.

Then Travis Rendell clanged one of those triangles that used to call cowboys in for chow. "Come and get it!"

"Let's sit together," Mary Lou said.


We sat at one of three long tables. Travis Rendell stepped up to a microphone on the stage at the front.

"Howdy everybody," he said. "I'm happy to have you all here tonight. We're gonna have some good eatin'. You've already been drinkin', but as long as you don't start singin' Danny Boy during dinner, it's all right."

Laughter.

"Now, my grandaddy had a saying. If God didn't want us to eat cows, he wouldn't have made 'em out of meat."

Laughter and a few hands clapping.

"Course, that's a message that ain't gettin' through to a lot of folks these days, and you all know about that. Things've been gettin' pretty darn unreasonable. But I'll tell you somethin' true. There's a change in the air."

Someone shouted, "That's right!" Which was followed by other voices of approval.

Rendell said, "We can feel it. We can smell it. And we can sure as heck eat it! So I invite you all to just sit back and enjoy—"

"The rape of the earth!" The voice came from behind us, at the door to the ballroom.

It was a young woman in a baggy sweatshirt. Long brown hair. If her face hadn't been scrunched up in wild anger she might have been pretty.

Sounds of disgruntlement rose in the ballroom.

Travis Rendell looked upset but not surprised. "Now's not the time, Danica."

A couple of the beefier waiters moved toward her.

"It's never the right time with you!" She sounded a little drunk.

Mary Lou Overstreet leaned over to me and whispered, "His daughter."

"Danica," Travis Rendell said, "we're having dinner. Let's talk another—"

"You all don't care!" Danica said. "You sit here in your fancy—"

One of the waiters took her arm. She yanked it away. "Don't you touch me!"

Rendell said, "It's all right, boys."

Mary Lou got up and started walking toward Danica.

"Stop it!" Danica said. "Just stop it!"

When Mary Lou was a few feet away Danica pointed at her. "Stay away from me!"

"Calm down, Danica," Mary Lou said. "Let's take it outside."

"You can all go straight to—"

"Outside," Mary Lou said.

Danica burst into tears, turned and ran out.

An uncomfortable silence draped the room.

Travis Rendell said, "Sorry about that, folks. You all know about my little family problem. I don't like airing dirty laundry in public, so why don't we try to forget it and return to the business at hand, which is to enjoy a fine meal together."

Baldwin Fish stood up and raised his glass of wine. "Let me say, on behalf of everyone, we're with you all the way, Travis."

Cheers and applause.

"Let's eat!" Travis Rendell said.

They started serving the salads.

Mary Lou said to me, "Danica was normal until she went off to Drake. They have a Caleb Crane cult there. You know about him?"

"A little," I said.

"Danny's mother died two years ago," Mary Lou said. "That's when she really went off the deep end."

The main course was New York strip, medium rare, with truffle mashed potatoes, grilled asparagus, and BBQ beans. Sophie got into a conversation with the woman sitting on her right. Mary Lou asked me about my cynicism bit and how I knew all that. I told her about my love of philosophy.

When the dessert was served—blueberry cobbler with vanilla ice cream—I was telling Mary Lou about Epicurus and the pursuit of pleasure, as represented by the fine meal we were having. I noticed someone had come into the ballroom. It was Jamie Anderson. He had a troubled look on his face. He went to where Travis Rendell was seated and whispered something to him. Rendell put his napkin on the table, got up, and left the room.

Jamie saw me. He gave me a motion with his head. I excused myself and went to him.

"What's up?" I said.

"The newspaper office was just bombed," he said, his voice cracking. "Mr. Peale was inside. He's dead."

T ravis Rendell came back in and went to the microphone. "Folks, I'm sorry to interrupt the proceedings, but I just got a report. The office of The Central Valley Dispatch was just firebombed. Reports are that Bill Peale is dead."

A hum of disbelief went up from the crowd.

"We all know what's going on," Rendell said. "There's a bunch of people around here who hate us. They'll poison our cows, they'll bomb the only honest newspaper within a hundred miles. They want to make us crawl under our blankets and cry. Well, we're not gonna do it. We're gonna fight!"

Cheers and applause.

"So I want you all to go home and keep safe. I've got our security team outside, watching the parking lot and all sides of the hotel."

Mary Lou walked Sophie over to me.

"I'm so sorry," Mary Lou said. "It was nice meeting you two. I hope you'll come see us again."

"We'll be back," I said.

Jamie Anderson was outside waiting to talk to us. "Somebody said Danica Rendell made a scene tonight."

"She did," I said.

"Think she might have something to do with this?"

I shook my head. "Something like this takes planning and expertise and secrecy."

"She might know who it was," Sophie said.

"After tonight, she'll no doubt be questioned," I said. "Any idea where we might find her?"

Jamie said, "Are you going to try to do something about this?"

"I liked your boss," I said. "I don't like whoever did this. So yeah, something."

"But what can you do?" Sophie asked as we drove away.

"I can ask questions," I said.

"But don't you have to get back?" Sophie said. "Ira's expecting you."

"Just a couple of days," I said. "I still want to find the kid who got beat up. Besides…"

"Yes?"

"We're on our honeymoon," I said. "Why cut that short? The cow pastures are beautiful this time of year."

"I'm living the dream," Sophie said.

Early the next morning, with Sophie in my arms under nice warm covers, my phone buzzed. It was Jamie.

"They made an arrest," he said.

"Already?" I said.

"A guy named Eddie Hastings. A Drake student."

"That was fast."

"I have the mug shot," Jamie said. "His face doesn't look so good. Thought that might interest you."

I sat up. "It does. Can you text it to me?"

"Sure. Hold on."

"What's up," Sophie said.

"They arrested a Drake student for the bombing," I said. "Jamie's going send—"

My phone bleeped. I looked at the picture.

"That's him," I said. "That's the guy from Gussie's."

"Wow," Jamie said. "What a story. Can I get a statement from you?"

"Wait a second..."

"What is it?"

"My little man is trying to tell me something," I said.

Sophie cocked her head and looked at me.

"What do you mean by that?" Jamie said.

"It's from a movie," I said. "Double Indemnity. Edward G. Robinson is an insurance investigator. He says he has a little man inside him who tells him when something isn't right."

Pause. "You think something's not right?"

"That's what he's saying. I know you have to write something for the paper. Can you leave out the part about me helping him out at Gussie's?"

"Mike, why?"

"I don't know," I said. "I need some time to find out."

"What are you going to do?"

"I don't know."

"Mike, I have to write this and put it online."

"Just hold back that one part," I said. "Let me work on this with you. Just a few days. Will you do that for me?"

Pause. "All right. But I want to know everything you find out."

"Of course," I said. "Stay tuned."

I ended the call. Sophie was still looking curiously at me.

"Little man?" she said.

"I never told you about him?"

"I think I would have remembered."

"He's very good," I said.

"Oh? How good?"

"Well, the first time I saw you he told me, 'This is the woman for you.'"

"He *is* good," Sophie said. "What is he telling you to do next?"

I kissed her.

"He's a plucky little fellow," she said.

"And he just gave me an idea."

I called Ira.

"How would you like to take on a new client?"

"Whoa!" Ira said. "What's going on?"

"Remember I told you about the fight at the diner?"

"How could I forget?"

"The guy who got beat up, he's been arrested for setting off a bomb in a newspaper office, killing the editor of the paper."

"What? Michael, what have you got yourself into?"

"It got into me," I said. "And I think they're railroading this kid."

"Why do you think that?"

"Call it a hunch."

"That's not enough," Ira said.

"Then I want to talk to him," I said. "Can I tell them you're going to represent him, and get in that way?"

"Each jail has its own rules," Ira said. "You may have to use some bluster."

"That's my meat."

"How well I know," Ira said. "All right, listen. If you get in and he consents to be repped by me, tell him he's going to be arraigned. I'm tied up for a couple of days, but I know a local attorney up there. I'll see if he's available to rep Eddie at the arraignment. If not, I'll tell you what to do."

"You always do," I said.

"Yeah," Ira said. "The trick is to get you to listen."

The police building looked more like an outlet store than a law enforcement enclave. A crowd bustled outside. I saw three news vans—from Bakersfield, San Jose, and Fresno. Film crews had cameras set up. A uniformed gray-haired man was talking in front of several microphones held by reporters.

Sophie followed me as we made our way around the knot toward the front doors. A young officer put his hand up.

"Can't go in there," he said.

I flashed him one of Ira's law cards. "Lawyer."

He frowned. "You don't look like a lawyer."

"You want to make that an issue?" I said.

"Who's she?"

"My confidential assistant," I said.

He looked confused. Always a good sign for me.

"Front desk," he said, and allowed us to pass.

There were a few people at the desk, which was manned by two police officers in front of monitors. A lot of chattering was going on.

We went up to the desk and waited until one of the officers looked at us with a scowl. "What do you want?"

"I'm here to see Eddie Hastings," I said, handing him Ira's card.

He gave it a cursory look.

"Can't be done," he said.

"Not only can it be done, it must be done."

"What?" It was more a put down than an inquiry.

"The Constitution still applies in Fresno County."

"We got a lot going on," he said. "You can wait over there and—"

"I understand you're busy," I said. "But denying access to a legal representative carries serious issues for your department. You don't want that, right?"

He looked like he wanted to tell me to go where it was hot.

"You can just wait right here." He returned to his monitor and tapped away at it.

I crossed my arms and put on Annoyed Look Number 7.

"Let's see how long this takes," I said to Sophie.

It took twenty minutes. Finally the officer disappeared through a back door. A few minutes later he came out with a senior officer.

"What's this about?" the senior said. He was a fireplug of a guy with a face made for staring down mad dogs.

I said, "I represent the lawyer who is going to represent Eddie Hastings. I want to see our client."

"You're trolling."

"We're asking," I said. "Surely you know that's allowed under California law, as long as we abide by the Rules of Professional Conduct. Your prisoner knows me. You tell him it's the guy who helped him in the fight at Gussie's Diner."

"What is that supposed to mean?"

"It means he'll want to see me," I said.

"Look, there's too much going on right now. Maybe come back tomorrow."

"You can't obstruct a legal representative," I said.

"You see if I can't."

In my sweet voice I said, "Officer, there's a bunch of reporters outside with cameras and microphones. I really don't want to make an issue out of this. I just want ten minutes to talk to your prisoner, and then I'll be on my way. We can keep this thing quiet and go on about our day. Or not."

At that point a commotion broke out in the reception area. Someone who looked and sounded like a reporter raised his voice at one of the desk officers. The senior officer sighed, shook his head, and said, "Follow me."

He led us through the door he'd come out of, but then stood in our way. "Who is this?" he said.

"This is my confidential assistant," I said.

"What does that mean?"

"She makes sure I remember things right," I said.

Sophie smiled at him. She can charm a thorn bush. This officer was no match. Without a word he led us past a room of cubicles and desks and a couple of uniformed police. Through another door we entered a hallway with two lockups. One had open bars. An old man in dirty clothes snored on the bench. Next to that was a door and with a cross-hatch safety window. The senior took a look through the window, gave a quick knock, then unlocked the cell.

Eddie was sitting on the bench, holding his knees, scrunched up as far in the corner as his body would allow. Sophie and I went in.

"I'll give you five minutes," the senior said.

"Ten," I said.

The officer slammed the door.

"Who are you?" Eddie said. His voice was weak. He had a black eye and purple bruises on his cheeks.

"Do you remember me Eddie? From Gussie's Diner?"

He gave me a look and said, "No."

"You had that fight. Dante was about to beat you to a pulp."

"That was you?"

"That was me," I said.

"Why are you here?"

"Do you have a lawyer?"

"No."

"Have you talked to the police?"

"I told them I didn't do it."

"Anything else?

"I said I didn't want to talk anymore. They told me somebody from the public defender's office was going to be here."

"I think you need a private lawyer," I said. "I work for one. His name is Ira Rosen, and he's first rate."

"Why would you do that?" Eddie said.

"Maybe because I think you're getting a raw deal."

He rubbed his temples. "I don't have any money."

"We can do this pro bono."

"What's that?"

"Free of charge."

"Free? Why?"

"Lawyers take cases for a lot of reasons," I said.

He thought about that for a moment. Then his eyes grew cold.

"You just want the publicity, don't you?" he said.

I sat on the end of the bench.

"Fair question," I said. "But I'll tell you, the last thing I want is publicity. I don't like being probed or poked or lied about. I don't trust the media. I offer our services because I have a thing about justice. It's been in pretty short supply lately."

"I'm not guilty," he said.

"I didn't ask if you were," I said. "Under the Constitution you have the right to be defended, no matter what."

"But I didn't do it!"

"Let's prove it," I said. "Where were you last night around ten p.m.?"

"I was home," he said. "Like I am every night."

"Where's home?"

"I rent a room near the campus."

"Can anyone vouch for you?"

He shook his head. "The woman I rent from, Mrs. Grande, is visiting her sister."

"What about a neighbor?"

"Not that I know of," Eddie said.

"Make a note to check that," I told Sophie. "Give me the exact times, Eddie. What were you doing before you got home?"

"I was at the school library."

"When?"

He rubbed his forehead. "Around five. I left and got a burrito from the AM/PM and brought it home."

"You have a receipt?"

"I used a credit card."

"You got home when?"

"Maybe six. Yeah, six. I watched TV and ate the burrito." He gave me a half smile. "I lead a very exciting life."

"Did you go out at all after that?"

"No."

"Did you call anybody?"

"No."

"Did anybody call you?"

He sighed heavily. "No."

"Did you send an email or text?"

"No."

"Did you log on to any sites?"

"No."

"What *did* you do?"

"I read a comic," Eddie said. "A Batman. I drank some tequila and fell asleep."

"What time was that?"

"I don't know. Maybe around ten."

I said, "According to the police report, you were arrested at 7:35 a.m."

"Yeah."

"All right, tell me what that fight with Dante was about."

The cell door opened. The senior officer said, "Time."

"That's not ten minutes," I said.

"Time's up." To Eddie he said, "Is this guy repping you?"

Eddie looked at me, at Sophie, at me again.

"Well?" the officer said.

"Yes," Eddie said.

I stood. "From now on, say nothing to anyone. Not police or reporters, not anybody. If they want to question you, insist on having me here. If they put somebody in this cell with you, don't trust him. Say nothing. Understand?"

Eddie nodded.

"You done now?" the officer said.

"Thank you for your kind indulgence," I said.

"Just get out of here," he said.

Outside the station reporters were jostling for position and shouting questions at the spokesperson, a woman in a crisp uniform looking like a substitute teacher in front of an unruly classroom.

A female reporter with a Channel 7 microphone made a beeline for me and Sophie.

"Excuse me," she said. "Are you related to the bomber?"

"Excuse *me*," I said. "He is only the accused."

"What's your part in this?" She had that terrier look reporters get when chasing a scoop that might get them noticed by the national desk.

"Nothing," I said.

"What were you doing inside?"

"Fighting a traffic ticket," I said.

The reporter frowned.

"I told him to just pay it," Sophie said. "But he won't listen."

"She's always telling me what to do," I said. "So annoying."

"You can sleep on the couch tonight," Sophie said.

The reporter issued a word that would not be allowed on the airwaves, and walked off.

I took Sophie's arm and led her toward Spinoza.

"Annoying am I?" she said.

"In a delightful way," I said.

When we got to my car an old man was waiting there. He was hunched over, wearing shades and a crumpled hat.

"Spare some change?" he said in a low growl.

"Who carries change anymore?" I said.

"Mike Romeo," he said, only now his voice was familiar.

"Jamie?"

He took off his shades.

"That's some getup," I said.

"Just keeping on the down low," he said. "Did you see him?"

"I did," I said. "We're going to represent him."

"You're kidding."

"I kid you not," I said.

"Why?"

"I don't think he did it."

"Why?"

"You're also supposed to ask who, what, and where questions."

Jamie pursed his lips. "I want to know everything."

"So do I," I said. "Look, somebody wanted the killing to be big and loud. But not for the obvious reason, not to make some anti-cattle-ranch, anti-beef statement. It's a distraction. I think it was to silence your boss about something else. Does that make sense?"

"Not yet," Jamie said.

"Was Bill Peale working on a story that might have rubbed some people the wrong way, in a big way?"

"Take your pick," Jamie said. "Bill took seriously his role as a journalist. He was always quoting the guy who said a journalist should afflict the comfortable, and comfort the afflicted. There's a lot of comfortable people around here who don't want to be afflicted."

"Can you name some?"

"Sure I can."

"How about making a list for me?"

"You really want to put a stick in that hornets nest?"

"Isn't that what your boss did?"

"Good point."

"Is there a name that you'd put at the top of the list?"

"The obvious one would be Jess Rendell, Travis's brother."

"Tell me about him."

"It's a well-known story around here. Their grandfather, Dac Rendell, was a Texan by birth and a Californian by conquest. He had a big cattle operation that was taken from him by one of the big conglomerates, so he came out to central California and started another ranch that grew during the Depression and really took off after the war. Dac had a son named Del, who took over in the 50s. Del had two sons. Jess and Travis. Jess was the older brother. But it was Travis who took an interest in all things cattle ranching. He's the smarter of the two. Jess wasn't exactly sterling in character. Bar fights, two failed marriages. So when it came time to choose a successor, Del chose Travis. Jess never got over that, I guess."

"And the older shall serve the younger," I said.

"How's that?"

"The Bible story. Jacob and Esau."

"The birthright thing," Jamie said.

"Jacob tricked Esau into selling his birthright for a bowl of stew. The worst negotiated deal in history. The Edomites, the descendants of Esau, were always mad at the Israelites, refused to help them, looked for ways to undermine them."

Jamie pondered that for a moment. "It fits. Jess went away for a long time but recently moved back to Fresno, with a boatload of money and nobody seems to know where it came from. So who knows what he's planning for Travis?"

The press conference at the station was breaking up.

"I should talk to him," I said. "Think you can find out where he lives?"

"I already know," Jamie said. "I'll get you the address."

"Good work," I said.

"I'm your intrepid reporter," Jamie said. "Keep in touch."

He turned and shuffled away.


"So what happens next?" Sophie said as we drove away.

"They'll arraign Eddie tomorrow," I said. "Then we get ready for trial."

"Wouldn't Eddie be better off with a local attorney?"

"If you have Ira Rosen defending you, you're better off by definition. There's nobody better on the law or in front of a jury. My job is to locate witnesses, maybe find Eddie an alibi."

"Maybe?"

"There's always the possibility he did it," I said.

"If you thought or Ira thought he did it, would you still represent him?"

"Of course," I said. "Every defendant has the right to a defense. Every prosecutor needs to be held to the burden of proof beyond a reasonable doubt. Drop that and soon enough we'll go back to the Inquisition. You've got the right to face your accusers. If you can't cross-examine, then lies go untested. Then you get the Salem Witch trials, like what they've tried to do to some Supreme Court nominees."

"Odious," Sophie said.

"Then it's not a matter of truth, it's a matter of power. The ends justify the means. Lie all you want. Find some lying witnesses. It's Josef Stalin. It's Torquemada. And Lady Justice weeping under her blindfold. Eddie Hastings is scared, he needs somebody to stand with him and make sure this isn't a railroad job, which I think it is."

"Did you ever think of becoming a lawyer?" Sophie said.

"I don't have the decorum for it," I said. "I can just imagine a judge saying, 'Mr. Romeo, are you trying to show contempt for this court?' And I'd say, 'No, Your Honor, I'm trying my best to conceal it.' Boom. Jail."

Sophie laughed.

"What about you?" I said. "What would you be doing if you weren't teaching?"

"When I was twelve I wanted to be an opera singer."

"No fooling?"

"My parents took me to see Carmen. I drove them crazy for a couple of weeks walking around the house singing the Habanera."

"In French?"

"I made up my own words," Sophie said. "That's what drove them crazy."

"I've never heard you sing," I said.

"Someday, Romeo. When the time is right."

"Let's make the time," I said.

"If you'll sing to me, too," Sophie said.

"You like the sound of cement mixers?"

"Maybe we should eat instead," Sophie said.


Casa Medina had six booths and three tables. Two of the booths and two of the tables were occupied. The aroma of fresh Mexican food filled the place.

A young woman told us we could sit anywhere we liked.

I asked Sophie what she'd prefer and she said a booth. My preference, too. The honeymoon was proceeding nicely.

The same young woman brought us menus and asked for our drink order. I suggested a margarita and Sophie agreed.

"We're getting along famously," I said.

"I'm not surprised," Sophie said. "Well, maybe a little."

"A little?"

"There's always some surprises with you," she said.

"I'm the gift that keeps on giving," I said.

She took my hand. "You are something all right."

A busboy delivered a basket of tortilla chips and a small bowl of salsa. The salsa was fresh, with just the right heat and dash of cilantro.

We munched and looked over the menu. The waitress brought our drinks, served in salt-rimmed glasses. Sophie ordered a chile relleno combo. I went for the beef chimichanga.

I lifted my glass. "A margarita, some tortilla chips, and thou beside me singing in the wilderness. Oh, wilderness is paradise."

"To paraphrase Omar Khayyam," Sophie said.

"He won't mind," I said. We clinked.

Ten minutes later a woman came in, alone. She went directly to an empty table, a four top, and sat.

I said, "Unless my eyes deceive me, Danica Rendell just came in."

Sophie turned for a quick look.

"I think you're right," she said. "She might recognize you."

"I don't think so. She wasn't looking at people when she crashed the party. She wanted to make a statement, is all."

"What do we do now?"

"We enjoy our meal," I said. "And watch."

Our food came. Danica drank water. Eventually she was served a meal. She picked at it, looking at her phone the whole time. The new form of companionship.

Sophie took another glance.

"I wish I could talk to her," she said.

"Why?"

"She's hurting."

"You know this how?"

"That outburst at the dinner. I don't think she was trying to convince anybody. I think she was trying to get her father's love."

"That's quite a diagnosis. What makes you think that?"

"I went through the same thing with my dad." Sophie looked at her plate. "There was a time we didn't care for each other. It was the typical adolescent thing. I was fifteen or so when he started to come down on me for certain things, mainly the music I was listening to. He didn't think it was uplifting. Tried to get me to stop. So what did I do? I went completely the other way and started listening to worse stuff. And believe me there's plenty of that out there."

"I believe you."

Sophie looked at me. "It got so bad that I left home for a while. I lived with a friend. Deep down I knew he loved me, but I wanted to feel it, I wanted to see it, wanted him to tell me. It took my knee for that to happen."

"Your knee?"

"I hurt it playing volleyball. I needed arthroscopic surgery. I was in the hospital for half a day, in recovery, and he came to see me. Dad doesn't show much emotion, but when he took my hand tears started rolling down his face. Then I started crying. And then we were embracing. A nurse had to come over and break it up. He begged me to come home. He said things would be different. And I said they would for me, too. I think Danica just wants to go home."

"Now you are the onion," I said.

Just then a man in a suit and tie came in, looked around, and went over and sat at Danica's table. She put her phone down and the two started talking.

"This is interesting," I said. "A man who looks like an accountant or a lawyer just sat down with Danica."

Sophie looked. "What do you suppose that's about?"

"No idea," I said. "I just find it interesting. I wouldn't have pictured her with a guy like that."

"Who knows?" Sophie said. "There was a time I didn't picture me with a guy like you."

"I warned you," I said. "Now you're stuck with me."

"So far, so good." She scooped up some rice and beans and took a bite.

"I've got an idea," I said. "It's time you got some training in surveillance."

"Cool," Sophie said.

"First question is, who should we follow? We could follow Danica, but that probably would not reveal anything about the man. On the other hand, if we follow the man, that may reveal something about them both."

Danica and the man were still talking when we left. The man hadn't ordered any food.

We got in Spinoza.

"Surveillance is ninety-five percent waiting," I said.

"So it helps to have a good companion," Sophie said.

"You lucky girl," I said.

"Nice flip."

I cleared my throat. "Now, when he gets into his car, two things. First, try to memorize his plate, if we're close enough to see it. Take a picture and we might be able to zoom in on it. The trickiest part is following. It's not like in the city."

"Wouldn't it be easier? Not as many cars here."

"That's what makes it harder. It's easier for the mark to spot somebody behind him. We have to keep distance, and that increases the chance of losing him. It doesn't help that Spinoza is a classic Mustang. If I know I'm going to follow somebody, I usually rent a car."

"We should have come in my Nissan."

"From now on, if we go out together, that's what we'll do."

Spinoza's a convertible. I put the top on.

About five minutes later the guy came out, alone.

"Here we go," I said.

He went to a car several spaces away. When he backed out I saw it was a black sedan. It had four interlocking circles on the back, the Audi logo. I couldn't make out the plate.

Sophie was ready. She took a picture.

The sedan headed for the exit.

I followed.

The Audi turned right into the main drag. I slowly made the same turn.

He was about a hundred feet in front of us.

"I can make out the plate," Sophie said, looking at her phone.

"Uh-oh."

"What?"

"He just went through a light. We have to stop. That's another hazard in long-distance tailing."

I stopped at the light. The sedan kept going. The road curved around and I lost sight of him.

The light changed. I gave Spinoza extra gas. But when we came around the curve there was no sedan in sight.

"Lost him," I said.

"No," Sophie said. "Look." She pointed to an Arco station on the right. The sedan was there. The guy was starting to pump gas.

I kept driving.

"Don't you want to stop?" Sophie said,

"This is a drive-past situation. If a mark thinks he might be tailed, you relieve him of that thought by driving on. We'll pull up over here and hope he comes out going in the same direction."

I stopped at the curb in front of a nail salon. Three minutes later I saw the sedan in my rearview mirror, coming our way.

"Kiss me," I said.

"Really?" Sophie said.

I reached over and pulled her to me and planted a major league kiss on her. And listened for the sedan passing by.

"Time to follow again," I said.

"I get it," Sophie said. "Make it look like we're busy, throw him off."

"I just wanted to kiss you," I said. "But that, too."


We followed him downtown. He pulled into the lot of a two-story office building. I stopped across the street.

"Now what?" Sophie said.

"We wait five minutes," I said. "Then you can earn your pay."

"What pay is that?"

"You're married to me, aren't you?"

"You have such a way of explaining things," she said.

"My gift," I said. "Go over to the lobby and see if there's a directory. Take a picture of it."

"What if there's a security guard?"

"Building this size, in this town, I doubt it. But if there is, use your charm."

"Thank you," she said.

We waited a few more minutes, then Sophie walked across the street. I watched her walk. It was the best part of the day.

She went in, came out a minute later, got back in the car.

"No guard," she said.

She showed me the picture on her phone. The directory had several names. There was also a CPA, a dentist, a chiropractor, a nail beautician, and the Law Office of Gerry McCracken.

"Look up the law office," I said.

Sophie worked her phone. "Here's the website."

"Does it list the attorneys?"

"Yes." She brought up the page. The first photo was Gerry

McCracken. He wasn't the guy. But scrolling down we found him.

His name was Grover Hawthorne.

> Mr. Hawthorne is an expert on the foundations of city land use authority through the constitutional police power; the basis for challenging public agency decisions; the requirements for and relationships between general plans, specific plans, zoning and subdivision regulations and development agreements; and basic environmental review requirements under the California Environmental Quality Act.

"Now why would a land use lawyer be meeting with Danica Rendell?" I said.

"Maybe it's personal," Sophie said.

"Like they're a couple? Those two?"

"Look at us," Sophie said. "Who would have guessed?"

"You have a point," I said. "Maybe I'll—"

A cop car pulled up behind us, light bar flashing.

The cop got out. I watched him in my side-view mirror.

"Now this is interesting," I said.

"What is?" Sophie said.

"I know this guy." It was the cop from Gussie's who wouldn't talk to me. Jacobsen. "Get ready to record this."

Sophie pulled the phone to her lap.

Officer Jacobsen stepped into my sightline.

"Afternoon, Officer," I said.

"License and registration please," he said.

"What is this for?" I said.

"License and registration."

"But this isn't a traffic stop," I said. "I was parked."

"Don't make this hard," Jacobsen said.

"Nothing hard about it," I said. "Since this isn't a traffic stop, you need reasonable suspicion of a crime. If you don't, I'm not obligated to produce anything. That's California law."

"What are you doing here?"

"I'm not obligated to answer."

He took a step back. "Please get out of the car, sir."

"I like this car," I said. "I like sitting in it."

"You're resisting an officer," he said.

"No, I'm educating an officer. And I'll make you a deal, Officer Jacobsen. Go your merry way and I won't post the video my assistant is making, nor send it to your superior."

For a moment he had the look of somebody who wanted to draw his weapon and kill both of us.

He didn't say another word. He went back to his car, got in, and drove away.

"You're making yourself very popular in this town," Sophie said.

"It's what I do," I said.

We went back to the Somber Sloth, which was like returning to a hospital room. No sunlight streaming through the windows. No view of the mountains or the sea. I was homesick. The only thing making it bearable was Sophie.

I called Ira and told him about the McCracken firm and Grover Hawthorne. I could hear him working the keyboard.

"Land use," Ira said. "And it looks like they're active in local politics."

"Can you cross-check them with the name Rendell?" I said.

"Hang on."

I hung on.

"Nothing turns up," Ira said. "You have a theory?"

"Not yet," I said. "Just data."

"I've got a lawyer for the arraignment tomorrow," Ira said.

"His name is Sonny Kemp. You can meet him outside the courtroom."

"How will I know him?"

"You can't miss him," Ira said. "He's built like a bowling ball, moves like a ferret, and I'm willing to bet his suit doesn't quite fit."

"Is this supposed to inspire confidence?" I said.

"Don't let looks fool you," Ira said. "Just do what he says."

After the call, Sophie and I sat on the bed and looked at the four walls.

I got up and said, "I'll be right back."

"Don't linger," Sophie said.

I went downstairs. Elena was outside the office, plucking weeds from one of the flower beds.

"Good afternoon," I said.

"Oh, hello." She straightened and wiped her forehead with the back of her hand. "Is everything all right?"

"The room is excellent," I said. "I was just wondering where two people might go to get out a little, maybe take in a view."

She smiled. "Two people in love?"

"You have us pegged," I said.

"A view, you say?"

"Is there such a place?"

She smiled. "Well now, there's a little spot I only let my best guests know about. It might suit your purposes."

"I'd love to hear about it," I said.

"Let me show you."

And that's how Sophie and I ended up sitting on two lawn chairs on the roof of the Somber Sloth, looking out at an expanse of fertile agricultural land, with the grand Sierra Nevada mountains in the distance.

"Do I know how to show a lady a good time, or what?" I said.

"Innovative, at the very least," Sophie said.

We had a bucket of complimentary popcorn between us, courtesy of Elena, and sipped two cans of Coke from the vending machine. The breeze was favorable and the scent of citrus was in the air.

I said, "If you had a day to spend doing anything you want, anywhere you want, and I was along for the ride, what would it be?"

"That's quite a question," Sophie said. "Can I go back in time? I'd love to see the opening night of As You Like It at The Globe and talk to Shakespeare afterward."

"What would you say?"

"I'd say keep on doing what you're doing and I'll tell kids in the future all about you."

"And what if you were time bound?"

She looked out at the horizon. "I think I'd go to Florence and spend hours looking at Michelangelo's David. And then to Trattoria Mario for their Steak Florentine."

"Ah, wonderful," I said. "But I can save us some money."

"Oh?" she said, taking a sip of Coke.

"Sure. You can look at me and then have chile rellenos."

She almost snorted Coke out her nose.


When we got to the courthouse the next morning, a couple of news vans were on the scene. Just outside the entrance a neatly dressed woman with long, ash-blond hair held a microphone. She was heatedly jawing with a guy holding a clipboard next to a TV camera.

Sophie and I walked on by and through the doors. We had to put our stuff on a conveyer belt and got waved through the security gate by a deputy who looked long past retirement age.

We got our things on the other side and took the elevator to the third floor where the arraignment court was.

The corridor had benches, and on the benches was a collection of anxious folks, relatives of the various arrestees, waiting for the courtroom doors to open. It seemed like a lot of people, then it occurred to me that some of these might be friends of the late Bill Peale.

No one fitting Ira's description of Sonny Kemp was in the hallway. The only one who looked like an attorney was a guy in a slick gray suit and the tightest, neatest coif of hair this side of the New York mafia. A briefcase sat by his feet. He thumbed his phone.

We found a spot on a bench.

"I guess courthouses are the same all over," Sophie said.

"Filled with desperation and hope," I said.

"What's going to happen in there?"

"They'll bring up the arrestees one by one. The judge'll read them their rights and ask for a plea, then talk bail. Then they'll set a date for a preliminary hearing. It's like the kickoff in a football game."

"Did you ever play football?"

I shook my head. "I was a chess man in college."

"Were you good?"

"Very."

"What opening did you favor?"

"That's a very intelligent question."

"My dad taught me chess," Sophie said. "I remember the Ruy Lopez."

"That's a fine, classic opening," I said. "I liked the King's Gambit."

"Why that?"

"Because it's aggressive," I said.

Sophie smiled. "That fits."

"Bobby Fischer liked it, and Paul Morphy."

"Who's Paul Morphy?"

"One of the great chess geniuses," I said. "Played in the mid-1800s. He was a child prodigy."

"Like you were."

"I had my moments," I said.

The elevator doors opened and out popped a squat man in a rumpled blue suit and cowboy boots with silver tips. He was bald on top with bushy gray hair on the sides that looked like it fought combs, and won. He was carrying a Gladstone briefcase.

He looked up and down the corridor.

I stood and walked toward him. He saw me and smiled.

"You must be Mike," he said.

"I was about to say you must be Sonny," I said.

"Right as rain on a dry patch," he said, extending his hand. His grip was iron.

Sophie was behind me. "This is my wife, Sophie," I said.

He shook her hand. "I am charmed. I like tall people. It's what I'd be if I was stretched out. Let's go over here and talk."

He led us to the end of the hall near the water fountain.

"Ira filled me in," Sonny said. "I talked to Eddie in the lockup, told him what's going on. They're going to charge Eddie with first-degree murder, special circumstances, with an LWOP sentence. That's life without parole. We'll plead not guilty and I'll get a copy of the complaint and pester the DA for the police report. After that we can talk a little about what's happening. There will be no bail."

"How is he?" I said.

"Scared as all get out," Sonny said. "I talked him down as best I could. Told him about how lucky he is to have Ira repping him. He wanted to know about you and I said we hadn't met yet, but that if Ira vouches for him, that's as good as gold on a Tiffany ring. And—" he looked at Sophie—"you've brought a diamond along for good measure."

"You're very kind," Sophie said.

"I'll mention that to my wife," Sonny said. "Been forty years together. How long you kids been married?"

"Four weeks," I said.

"And two days," Sophie said.

"Young love!" Sonny said. "Ain't it grand?"

"You need anything from us?" I said.

"Just a promise that you'll be happy together," he said.

"Done," I said.

People started for the door.

"Go on in and have a seat," Sonny said. "It's show time."


The courtroom filled up quickly. At the counsel tables sat two lawyers, a man and a woman. They each had a stack of files in front of them.

The clerk told everybody to stand and called the proceedings to order, Judge Allen Stevenson presiding. The judge came in and took his seat at the bench. He looked like Patton's younger brother, only with less compassion.

Three arrestees were arraigned. Judge Stevenson rattled off the legal language in clipped tones. But when he called Eddie's case, and Sonny jumped to his feet in the front row of the gallery, he barely suppressed a smile.

"Haven't seen you for a while, Mr. Kemp," Judge Stevenson said.

"Living large, Your Honor," Sonny said as he strode through the gate.

"Still raising chickens?"

"Oh yes," Sonny said. "Clucks for bucks. I'll bring you some eggs."

"Just bring me a plea," Stevenson said.

A bailiff the size of a zeppelin led Eddie into the courtroom from a side door. He was in jailhouse blues and shackled at the wrists. He looked like a dog that'd just been smacked on the butt.

And then a burst of voices erupted.

"Killer!"

"Hang 'im!"

And other such sentiments.

The judge slammed his palm on the bench. "None of that! Our lockup is big enough for all you people, understand?"

The shouts became a quiet grumble, then melted into silence.

Sonny went and stood next to Eddie. "Your Honor, Mr. Hastings is represented by Ira Rosen of Los Angeles. I'm here on his behalf. We will waive a reading of the complaint and statement of rights, and enter a plea of Not Guilty."

"Mr. Hastings," the judge said, "have you conferred with Mr. Kemp?"

Eddie nodded.

"Please respond verbally, Mr. Hastings."

"Yes." Eddie's voice was barely above a whisper.

"You understand what you're being charged with?"

"No."

"You don't understand?"

"I didn't do it," Eddie said.

"You wish to plead Not Guilty?"

"I didn't do it."

"That's all, Mr. Hastings. Your plea of Not Guilty is entered. Now, you have the right to a trial within sixty calendar days, unless you waive that right. Has Mr. Kemp explained that to you?"

Eddie looked at Sonny. Sonny nodded.

"Yes," Eddie said.

"If you waive this right, this doesn't mean your case is forgotten or ignored. Do you understand that?"

Eddie nodded.

"Out loud, please," the judge said.

"Yes."

"Do you wish to waive your statutory right to a speedy trial."

"I don't know what any of this means," Eddie said.

"Mr. Kemp, please confer with your client."

Sonny started whispering to Eddie. More grumbling in the courtroom. It was good no torches or pitchforks were being handed out.

Finally, Sonny said, "Ready, Your Honor."

"Mr. Hastings, do you understand what your lawyer just explained to you?"

He barely got the word *Yes* out when he started to cry.

Sonny put his arm around Eddie. "Give us a moment, Your Honor."

"Cry like a baby!" someone shouted.

The judge said, "Take that man out of the courtroom!"

The bailiff moved toward to the gallery. A man got up and started for the door, muttering, "Okay, okay, okay."

Sonny said, "Let's try it again, Your Honor."

"Mr. Hastings, look up here," the judge said. "Do you understand your right to a speedy trial?"

"Yes," Eddie said, barely audible.

"Do you waive that right?"

"Yeah."

"Counsel join?"

"Yes," Sonny said.

"People on bail?"

The Deputy D.A. argued for no bail. Sonny argued that Eddie had no record and was no threat to the community.

The judge denied bail.

They set a date for the preliminary hearing, and the bailiff took Eddie back through the side door.

.  .  .

I n the hallway we conferred with Sonny Kemp. He sat us on a bench and put his briefcase on it.

"He's not communicative," Sonny said. "He's obviously depressed. Like he's given up. I have to show you this."

Sonny took a document from his briefcase and handed it to me.

"The police report," Sonny said. "Not good news. There's an eye witness. Santiago Cruz, fix-it shop owner. His store's across the street from the newspaper office."

"Did he ID Eddie?" I said.

"His car," Sonny said. "Got the license plate."

I slapped the report across my hand.

"Can I talk to Eddie?" I said.

"He's in the lockup," Sonny said. "Lower level."

I stood. "Straight up, you think Eddie could have done this?"

"Every defendant starts out saying he didn't do it. You dig a little and pretty quick you get to know who's lying. You can see it in his eyes, hear it in his voice, you know, like the little boy who says he didn't take a cookie even though he's got crumbs on his mouth. You can even eventually tell who the practiced liars are. But Eddie, I don't get him. He says he didn't do it, but then clams up. Won't say more. I can't tell if he's hiding something or just giving up."

Sophie said, "If he's innocent, he's got to be scared out of his mind."

"Same if he's guilty," Sonny said.

He shook our hands and checked his watch, then bid us goodbye.

. . .

W e took the elevator to the lower level. A desk deputy in front of the lockup gave us a surly look. I showed him my ID and Ira's card and asked to see Eddie.

"Only attorneys," he said. He was bored and tired, like he was he'd been doing duty at the gates of Hades for centuries.

"Or agents of the attorney," I said. "Article I, Section 15 of the California Constitution. I am that agent. I am registered as such with the California Bureau of Prisons. It'll take you sixty seconds to confirm that. Thirty if you can type fast."

He looked at Sophie. "Who's she?"

"My assistant and amanuensis."

"Amanu what?"

"Someone who writes down what is said. Like a court stenographer."

He pondered, then said, "Wait here." He got up and went through a side door, trying to show us some swagger.

"Maybe you shouldn't use such big words," Sophie said.

"I consider it continuing education," I said. "Let people learn a little something instead of just warming their chairs. That guy is now using some brain cells that have been dormant for years."

"Don't expect a thank you note," Sophie said.

"A look of resignation on his face will be thanks enough."

And that's exactly the look he had when he returned.

"This way," he said.


H e took us to an interview room, which was a little bigger than a size 10 shoebox. There was a small table and two chairs. He told us to wait. I had Sophie sit at the table. She took out her phone to record the interview.

Another deputy brought Eddie in, sat him in the other chair.

"How long you need?" the deputy asked me.

"How about ten?" I said.

"We got a lot of guys to move around."

"I'll do my best."

The deputy left, closing the door behind him. Eddie looked ready to crawl in a hole and die.

"How you holding up, Eddie?" I said.

"Not great, man," he said. "Who's she?"

"This is Sophie," I said.

"Hello, Eddie," Sophie said.

"Why is she here?"

"She's going to record our conversation," I said. "We need your permission to do that."

Eddie closed his eyes. "Whatever."

"Is that a yes, Eddie?" I said.

"Yeah."

I nodded to Sophie and she started recording.

"Have you said anything to an officer or detective since you got here?" I said.

"No."

"Did they try to question you?"

"No."

"What was that fight with Dante about?"

"What does it matter?"

"Everything matters," I said. "So why did he beat you up?"

Eddie looked at the table and shrugged.

"What aren't you telling me, Eddie?"

Pause. "I don't want to talk about it."

"I don't care what you want," I said. "Talk."

"Come on, man," Eddie said.

"You want representation or not?"

He sighed and looked at the ceiling. "All right, look, I was at the protest by the freeway and Dante told me to leave."

"Why?"

"I don't know. He doesn't like me."

"So you've had run-ins with him before?"

"Not much."

"What was different this time? Why did he follow you to Gussie's?"

"He's just crazy," Eddie said. "I thought he wouldn't do anything in front of Gussie's. I guess I was wrong."

"What did you say to him when he got out of his truck?"

"I don't remember," Eddie said.

"I don't buy that, Eddie," I said. "Think harder."

"I don't know! Just told him he wasn't thinking right and leave me alone."

"Thinking right about what?"

"Just not thinking at all, okay? He's like that."

"Come on, Eddie."

There was a moment of fire in his eyes. Then it went out and he lowered his chin to his chest. "That's all I got."

I didn't have time to prod him more on that.

"The police report says there's a witness who saw your car around ten o'clock, downtown."

Eddie's head snapped up. "He's lying! Who is it?"

"A store owner across the street from the office," I said.

"Big fat liar!"

"So you're saying your car was with you at home?"

"Of course it was."

"Could it have been stolen and then put back?"

Eddie looked at the ceiling, as if searching for an opening to a parallel universe.

"So it is possible, right?" I said.

Eddie's skinny body started to shake. He closed his eyes, shook his head. A pitiful note escaped his throat. And then he was crying.

"Why is this happening to me?" he said.

I was about to answer when I felt Sophie's hand on my arm.

"Eddie," she said, "do you have family we can contact for you? Close friends? Your landlady, maybe?"

Eddie groaned. "She's gonna kick me out."

"How about family?" Sophie said.

Eddie rubbed his eyes. "My dad and I don't get along so good."

"I've been there," Sophie said. "Sometimes a thing like this can bring people together, if you're willing to try."

Eddie said nothing. He wiped his nose with the back of his hand. Sophie got a tissue from her purse and gave it to him.

"Any friends?" Sophie said. "Are you seeing anybody?"

"I don't want to talk anymore," he said. "I didn't do it, that's all you need to know. When can I get out of here?"

"You've been denied bail," I said. "It's going to be a while."

He whimpered and pressed the tissue to his eyes. "I'm scared of jail."

"You'll get through it," I said.

"Maybe I should just hang myself."

"Don't even joke about that," I said.

"Think I'm joking?"

"You better be," I said. "You'll get through this. I've been in the joint myself a few times."

"You have?"

"Yeah. And when you come out of this, you'll be stronger."

He dabbed his eyes. "What if I don't come out of it?"

"Thinking that way won't help," I said. "You can control your thoughts. Some of the best thinkers and writers of all time did their best thinking and writing inside a prison."

Eddie dropped his head again. He looked like a boxer who couldn't get up for Round Ten.

"Just tell me you'll try, Eddie. That's all I want to hear. Sophie and I and the best lawyer in L.A. are on your side. You owe us that much. Will you try?"

After a long moment, Eddie said, "Okay."

"Good," I said. "You'll be a stoic yet."

"A what?"

"A survivor," I said.

A s we drove away from the jail, Sophie said, "I have a theory."

"Let's hear it," I said.

"I think what happened between Dante and Eddie may have had something to do with a woman."

"That's quite a theory. You have a basis for it?"

"Did you see his reaction when I asked if he was seeing anybody?"

"He cut us off," I said.

"There was a flash in his eyes, like I'd hit a nerve and he didn't want us to see it."

"Not bad," I said. "We'll throw it in the stew pot, as Joey Feint used to say." Joey Feint was a private investigator I worked for before I left New Haven for good. He taught me a lot of things, including how to pick locks and read body language. All information and clues gathered, he would throw into his "stew pot." He'd let it simmer, taste every now and then, determine what ingredient was missing. Then he'd go find that ingredient.

A clash over a woman was a promising spice.

"Let's go shopping," I said.

"Shopping? For what?"

"The truth."

.   .   .

W e drove to the middle of town. The Central Valley Dispatch office was boarded up and criss-crossed with yellow police tape. Directly across the street was Chop's Shop–Used Appliances and Repairs. We parked in front and went in. A little bell tinkled on the door.

The place was stuffed with random appliances—coffee makers, refrigerators, microwaves, washing machines—all with bright yellow tags hanging from them with string. The smell of dust, rust, and Windex scented the air.

Behind a messy counter was a guy with glasses worn low on his nose, looking at what might have been a toaster oven. He was talking to a guy on the other side of the counter. They seemed to be discussing the relationship of price to condition. This is also called haggling.

"Let's do some browsing," I said to Sophie.

"We could use a blender," she said.

"A fine idea, Mrs. Romeo."

We strolled around until we found a shelf that had an old Hamilton Beach blender sitting on it. The yellow tag said $22.

"How's this look?" I said.

"Might do," Sophie said. "See if you can talk him down."

"Let's get him to talk first," I said.

We waited another minute. The haggling ended. The customer left the store. The bell tinkled.

We went to the counter, me carrying the blender like a football.

"Howdy," I said.

The counter man, mid-fifties, smiled. "Hello."

"Are you Chop?" I said.

He shook his head. "Santiago. Chop Grant started this place. Died a couple years ago. I worked for him."

"We're from out of town," I said. "Saw your place and thought we might find a blender. Isn't that right, honey?"

"That's right, sweetheart," Sophie said.

"She's always looking for a bargain," I said.

"You've come to the right place," he said.

"Sure looks like it," I said. "Say, what the heck happened across the street?"

"Oh, that's a big deal. A bomb went off."

"You gotta be kidding."

"No. That's a newspaper office. Boom!"

"Really?"

He nodded proudly. "I called the police."

"So this guy bombed the place in broad daylight?" I said.

"No, it was night."

"And you saw him through the window?" I said.

"His car was right in front of the office," he said.

"And you saw him with the bomb?" I said.

He frowned. The first glimmer of suspicion rippled in his eyes. "I saw his car."

"Boy," I said. "Good thing you were here."

"Anything else you need?" he said.

"Honey?" I said.

"I don't think so," Sophie said.

"Okay," I said. How about I take this off your hands for oh, say, fifteen bucks?"

He smiled then. He was back in his wheelhouse. "It's in perfect condition. I make sure of that."

"A break for a couple of out-of-towners, maybe?"

"You look like a nice couple," he said. "You can have it for twenty."

"Done."


We drove away with our blender and some questions.

"What did you think of his story?" I said.

"He seemed pretty happy to tell it," Sophie said. "Until you pressed him."

"Did you notice the hours of operation on the door?"

"I didn't."

"Closes at six. The bomb went off around ten. What was he doing there?"

"He could make something up."

"Look at the police report. Doesn't it say something about the license plate?"

Sophie looked at the sheets. "It says he took down the license plate number."

"If the car is parked lengthwise in front of the office, how does he see the license plate?"

"Ah."

"Be prepared to testify," I said. "You could turn into our star witness at the preliminary hearing."

"I never wanted to be a star," Sophie said.

"But you are," I said. "The brightest in my galaxy."

"Charmer."

I said, "How about using your own charm?"

"Meaning what?"

"How would you like to go undercover?"

"Me?"

"That group of anti-beefers who gather at the freeway. Drive over and go up and ask what this is all about, tell them you're interested in the issue, get them talking. See if they drop any info about the bombing, about Eddie. Don't be too obtrusive. Ease into it."

"Do I get a cool undercover name, like Mata Hari?"

"How about Surreptitious Sophie?"

"Hmm..."

"Syrup for short." I put my arm around her shoulders. "Because you're so sweet."

"Oh, man, you're really working it," she said.

"It's what I do," I said.

I dropped Sophie off at the motel so she could get her car. Then I drove to Rendell Ranch and asked the front desk if I might speak to Mary Lou Overstreet. The receptionist made a call, and two minutes later Mary Lou came out to greet me.

She tried to look pleasant, but it was clear recent events weighed heavily on her.

"I'm glad you came by," she said. "I need a break."

"From?" I said.

"I've been on the phone all morning arranging added security. We're all on high alert as you can imagine."

"Can I have a few minutes of your time?"

"All you want. Come with me."

She led me to her office. It had French doors that looked out at the cattle pens.

"That's my view every day," she said. "Reminds me why I'm here. I look out there and see the top of the American beef industry. I see people having barbecues and tailgate parties. I see people coming together. But I also see the craziness. And it's deadly."

"That's partly why I'm here," I said. "I wanted to make something clear to you and Mr. Rendell."

"Please," she said. "Have a seat."

She sat at her glass-covered desk and I parked on a leather chair. On her desk was a computer monitor, landline phone, a framed photo, some papers neatly stacked, and a cactus plant in a brick-red pot.

"Nice opuntia microdasys," I said.

"Excuse me?" Mary Lou said.

"Your bunny-ear cactus."

She looked at her plant, then back at me. "How do you know that?"

"Flowers and plants are a hobby of mine," I said. "And Latin."

"You speak Latin?"

"Some. Opuntia microdasys means small and prickly."

"Wow," she said.

Behind her, on the wall, was a diploma.

"Cornell grad, eh?" I said.

"The Ag school," she said. "Which is why Travis calls me A1."

"Like the steak sauce?"

"Because I was number one in my class," Mary Lou said with a grin. "But he does enjoy the double meaning. Where did you go to learn Latin?"

"Yale."

"You kicked our butts in football."

"Except the year you had Ed Marinaro."

"Who?"

"Before our time," I said. "It was 1971. Marinaro was a running back who should have won the Heisman Trophy. He went on to an acting career. He was on a show called Hill Street Blues."

"You're a fascinating person, Mr. Romeo."

"Or maybe I have too much time on my hands," I said.

"I doubt that very much."

I looked at the frame on her desk. Mary Lou turned it around.

"My daddy," she said.

He was a rugged looking man in a work shirt, arms crossed, not posing, almost like he was embarrassed having his picture taken.

"Man of the earth, looks like," I said.

"That's it exactly," she said. "Strong. And funny. Had all sorts of sayings. Like, love ain't fireworks, it's coffee at 5 a.m. and knowing when to shut up."

"My wife will like that one," I said.

She laughed. "And if you do wrong, make it right, and let the buffalo chips fall where they may."

"An honest man."

She turned the photo back to herself. "He had more integrity than any man I've ever known. Him and Travis Rendell."

A wisp of sadness swept over her face.

"But you are here with a purpose," she said.

"I am," I said. "The kid they arrested for the newspaper bombing—"

"I'm glad they got him."

"The lawyer I work for in L.A., he's going to defend him."

Silence. I could hear some cows mooing in the distance.

"I don't understand," Mary Lou said. "I thought he retained a lawyer, somebody out of Fresno."

"That was for the arraignment," I said. "The kid has retained us."

"How could that be? You only just got here."

I told her about the fight at Gussie's and going to see Eddie at the jail.

Mary Lou did not look happy. "Why on earth would you take his case?"

"Because I don't think he did it."

"What do you base that on?"

"Talking to him. And the way it went down. I don't think he's capable of something like that."

"Wow," she said.

"But I don't want you or Mr. Rendell to think this has anything to do with the anti-beef sentiment out there. It has to do only with the presumption of innocence."

"I do understand that," she said.

"Maybe you can help me out."

"How?"

"Anybody made threats to the ranch, anyone you can identify?"

She huffed. "I've got a whole file of threats, rants, hate mail and the like. Mostly anonymous."

"I wonder if I might have a look at it."

"I can make you a copy," she said. "I gave it to the private security firm I brought in. Travis wants me to ramrod this."

"Ramrod in the old cattle drive sense?"

She laughed. "Something like that. Anything else I can help you with?"

"I wonder if I might have a word with Mr. Rendell."

"Let's go."

S he walked us to Travis Rendell's office. She knocked on the door and a booming voice said, "Come in."

Travis Rendell sat behind a huge desk made from a felled tree. The edges were organic, roughly shaped. Tree rings swirled under a polished surface.

Mary Lou said, "Mr. Romeo would like to have a word with you."

"My pleasure," Rendell said. He came around the desk and shook my hand. "Nice to see you again." He was dressed in business casual, with boots and a belt buckle shaped like a wagon wheel.

"I'll leave you to it," Mary Lou said. "Let me know if there's anything else you need."

"Will do," I said.

She smiled and walked out.

Rendell offered me a seat. He sat behind his desk in a cowhide executive chair. "What can I do for you?"

"A lot's happened in the last few days," I said. "You probably know the lawyer I work for is representing Eddie Hastings in the bombing."

"I do," Rendell said. "Can I ask why?"

"The presumption of innocence for one thing."

"You think he's innocent?"

"I said presumed. The Constitution and all. And the Golden Thread."

"Golden Thread?"

"No man shall be convicted if there is reasonable doubt as to his guilt."

Rendell laced his hands behind his head. "You're a thoughtful man, Mike. I like that."

"I'm paid to think," I said. "And gather information. I'm trying to tie things together. There's a lot of resistance to your ranch."

He put his hands on the desk. "You don't have to tell me that. Mike, we take pride in running things the right way here. Lot of people think big operations like ours are all about squeezing every last dime, but that's not how we do things. These cows get treated better'n some people."

"How so?"

"Well, for starters, we keep the herd stress free. All those singing cowboys lullabying the cows on the prairie, that wasn't for show. A stressed animal doesn't eat right, doesn't gain proper weight. It affects the quality of the meat. I can tell when a hamburger's nervous. So we make sure they've got plenty of space, fresh water, steady diet. None of that cramming them into pens like sardines you see in some places."

"You need a lot of land for that."

"You got that right. We rotate the pastures so the land doesn't get overgrazed, let 'em feed on real grass when we can. When they're in the feedlot we got a nutritionist comes out to make sure their diet's balanced. Mostly corn, soybeans, and hay, with supplements to keep 'em healthy."

"Which makes those poisoned cows a mystery."

"Makes me sick to think about it, having them die that way.

We have a system that respects the cows. Curved chutes that allow for their natural movements so they don't panic."

"As the end draws nigh," I said.

"They give their lives to feed us. Least we can do is make sure they don't suffer."

"You have any guess as to how it happened, the poisonings?"

He shook his head. "We've got a security firm looking into it. We'll find the guy."

"How well did you know Bill Peale?"

"Pretty well. A good man. Trustworthy." He leaned forward. "Mike, I know you're doing your job and all, but if your guy did it I want him sent away for the rest of his life."

"Fair enough," I said. "I've asked Mary Lou for a list of the threats that have been made. Can you add anything?"

He gave me a long look. "You go ahead and do your job, Mike. We'll do ours. Meanwhile, I have a ranch to run."

"Thanks for your time," I said.

"Not a problem," Travis said, standing. "Maybe when this is all over we can have dinner sometime. With your lovely wife."

I stood and we shook hands. "Steak?" I said.

Travis Rendell laughed. "It ain't gonna be chicken nuggets."

I found my way out.

Only I took a detour. On an impulse, I pushed through a door marked *Employees Only*. It led to a ramp that took me down to a gravel path that ran along a huge cattle pen. Across the way a guy on a tractor chugged along, leaning out of the cab so he could look at the ground.

I kept on going toward a corrugated metal barn at the end of the path. The door was slightly ajar and I slipped in.

Sunlight poured through the slatted windows. It smelled like hay and old rubber in there.

Along the wall were stacks of bags stenciled with a logo and the word *Feed*. Also a bin of what I took to be silage, and if my educated nose was any guide it had an alfalfa base.

I went to the bags and patted the one on top. That was about as effective as kicking the tires on a new car. But it was something. I didn't know what I was looking for. I was just looking.

I heard a crunch behind me.

It was a sound that saved my life.

W hen someone intent on sticking you with a pitchfork is within ten feet, there's no time to think. Most people's survival instinct would have them putting their hands out or taking a step back, which only delays the inevitable by half a second.

In the cage I've been charged by many a fighter, and a move I perfected was the defensive fall-back-and-roll. That was for a flying fist or kick coming at me.

Now it was a five-pronged pitchfork in the hands of a guy built like a bull.

As I went down the weapon whizzed over me and impaled the bags.

I completed the roll and shot to my feet.

That bought me a second to make my next move.

If you can't run, you grab. And there was a beautiful flat-edged shovel leaning against one of the stalls.

I got to it just as the guy made his next thrust. I held the shovel in two hands. The tines of the pitchfork hit the wood handle and came to within an inch of my gut.

I pushed and twisted. The shovel scoop was on top. I slammed it into the guy's head.

He staggered, still holding the pitchfork. Now we faced each other like two gladiators in the arena.

"You're making a mistake," I said.

He bared his teeth like a wolf protecting its cubs.

I held up the shovel like a baseball bat. "Don't try."

For a second it looked like he did let a thought intrude, but in the next moment his eyes went feral, and I knew he was going to come at me.

"Fredo!" The voice boomed from the entrance.

My attacker stayed put. The guy who yelled was lean and well-proportioned, in a tight black T-shirt and black pants. He had black hair, too, which was also tight on his head. He wore a duty belt with a sidearm.

"Put that down," the guy said.

Fredo looked at me like he really wanted to give me another go. But he obeyed the order and lowered the pitchfork.

Another black-clothed fellow rushed in. He was also in good shape.

Black Hair said, "Take Fredo out of here."

The second guy motioned for Fredo to join him. Fredo shot me a dagger look, then threw the pitchfork down, hard. He stormed to the second guy and walked past him. The guy followed.

Black Hair said, "Who are you?"

"I'm a guest." I tossed the shovel on the ground. "Being attacked with a deadly weapon is not how you treat guests."

"You're not authorized to be in here."

"Then give me a sharp rebuke and I'll be on my way."

He whipped out the sidearm. It was thick, like a Taser. He didn't point it at me, just let me see he was ready to.

"We're gonna straighten this out," he said.

I could read the yellow script on the left breast of his shirt —*Snyder Security*.

"You Snyder?" I said.

"That's right," he said. "Who are you?"

"Name's Mike, and I was just talking to Mary Lou Overstreet and Travis Rendell."

"Why are you in here?"

"I was taking a stroll, looking the place over."

"Why?"

"Interested in the workings."

"Did you get permission?" Snyder said.

"Not exactly." I took a step.

He pointed the Taser at me. "Don't move."

"That's not necessary," I said.

"Don't test me. Just stay where you are." He took out a phone with his left hand and thumbed it, put it to his ear.

"Got a guy down here. Says his name's Mike and he's a guest. There's been an incident...ask Rick...sure."

He put the phone away.

"We're gonna wait a few minutes," he said.

"You want to tell me why a guy tried to kill me with a pitchfork?"

"Just wait. No talking."

"We might as well talk," I said. "No use wasting time."

He shook his head.

"We can exchange ideas," I said. "Are you into metaphysics?"

"Just shut up."

"I mean, haven't you ever wondered why things exist? Or whether we have free will?"

"You're a weirdo," he said.

"Just different," I said. "But we all are, in a way. We're unique beings in this mysterious universe."

"Don't make this hard."

"Thinking deeply *is* hard," I said. "But ultimately rewarding."

He rolled his eyes. "I may Tase you just to shut you up."

"That wouldn't look good on your resumé," I said.

He said nothing.

"You getting any further on the poisoned cows?" I said.

"We're not talking," he said.

"What's your favorite movie?"

"Jeez."

"I like *Sergeant York* with Gary Cooper. Ever seen it?"

Nothing.

I said, "True story, about Medal of Honor winner Alvin York in World War One. He took out a German machine gun nest single handed. He was a crack shot with a rifle. You'd like it."

Snyder's phone buzzed. "Yeah?...Okay."

He put the phone away. "We're going to see Mr. Rendell."

"Yippee ki-yay," I said.

S nyder kept his distance as we walked back to the main building, keeping his Taser out. We went in the same door I'd come out of, and down to Travis Rendell's office. The door was open.

Travis Rendell stood behind his desk. To his right was a serious looking man in a gray suit. On his other side was Mary Lou Overstreet, arms folded across her chest.

"That'll be all, Vance," Travis Rendell said. Snyder holstered his weapon, reluctantly it seemed to me.

"Close the door, please," Travis said.

Snyder left.

Travis said, "Mike, this is Bruce Butler, our legal counsel."

The man in the gray suit gave me the stink eye.

"Now what in God's green acre is this all about?" Travis said.

"Just your average pitchfork attack," I said.

"What were you doing in there?" Travis said.

"The door was open," I said. "I was having a look around."

"Why?"

"To gather information," I said.

"That's not your concern," Travis said.

Mary Lou Overstreet said, "Mike, that was rude of you."

"You're right," I said. "And I apologize."

Lawyer Butler spoke up. "If I may. You are representing the man who bombed the newspaper, isn't that right?"

"Accused," I said. "He hasn't been convicted."

"Bill Peale was a friend of the Ranch," Butler said.

"So you naturally want his murderer brought to justice, right?"

"Of course, but—"

"If the wrong guy is convicted, the real killer gets off."

"Mr. Romeo," Butler said, "do you intend to make an issue about what just happened? Because you were trespassing. You had no right to be in that barn. Any security breach is—"

"You don't have to go on," I said. "I'm not interested in suing you."

"Would you be willing to sign a waiver to that effect?" Butler said.

I looked at Travis. "How about I give you my word?"

"That's not good enough," Butler said.

Travis Rendell put his hand up. Butler stopped talking.

"It's good enough for me," Travis said. "Leave us, Bruce."

"I wouldn't advise that," Butler said.

"Duly noted," Travis said. He gave Butler a slap on the shoulder.

Butler pursed his lips and started for the door.

"No worries, counselor," I said.

The lawyer went out the door.

"He's paid to worry," Travis said. "Mary Lou, you want to add anything?"

She shook her head. "We like you, Mike. But we've got to

be so careful."

"Agreed," I said.

"Give us a moment," Travis said.

Mary Lou nodded. She paused to shake my hand. "No hard feelings."

"None at all," I said.

She left.

"Have a seat," Travis said.

"The fellow who attacked you is, um, mentally challenged. His name is Alfredo Neruda. We call him Fredo. He loves cows, I mean, a lot, so was pretty shaken up by the poisonings. He probably went a little crazy when he saw you in there."

"I've been known to go a little crazy myself," I said.

Travis nodded like he understood. "I know you think your client is innocent."

"It looks that way to me," I said.

"You think maybe it could have been one of those crazies out at the college?"

"You include Danica in that?"

He shook his head. "You're right to ask. But she wouldn't do something like that, or even be involved with the one who did it. She's headstrong. She's a Rendell. But she's got a soft heart. She got that from her mother."

"You talk to her much?"

"Not as much as I'd like," Travis said, a sad look in his eye. "I wish I'd spent more time with her when she was growing up. When she was little she used to come in here and I'd stop whatever I was doing and play bronco with her. I'd put her on my back and get on all fours and do a little bucking. She'd grab hold of a hunk of my shirt and hang on like a champion bronc buster."

He paused then and tapped his desk with his fingers.

"When her ma died she was sixteen, and that changed her. Changed both of us. She fell in with the anti-beef brigade. As you saw at the banquet."

"Has she ever mentioned Caleb Crane?"

"Ah, Crane. He's some kind of hero to them. I know he's been buying up land all over the U.S. of A."

"He ever make overtures to you?"

"One of his lawyers talked to Bruce. Bruce told him in no uncertain terms that Rendell Ranch was not for sale."

"You know about the McCracken law firm?"

"Sure," Travis said. "What about 'em?"

"My wife and I were eating at Casa Medina and saw Danica there. One of the lawyers from the firm, a guy named Grover Hawthorne, came in and talked to her."

Travis leaned over and put his elbows on the desk. "That's interesting. They're legal counsel for this guy Baldwin Fish. I think you met him."

"Briefly," I said. "At the banquet."

"He's the perfect California politician," Travis said. "Talks out of both sides of his mouth and his butt at the same time."

"How about your brother?" I said.

"Jess? He's no killer. He's a cattleman. A stupid, bitter one, but he's still a cowboy."

"You in touch with him at all?"

"Nah. I heard he's in Fresno. But we haven't spoken in years. You have family, Mike?"

"Only my wife," I said.

"No folks?"

"Deceased."

"Ah, sorry. I miss my folks every day."

"Me, too."

He stood and came around the desk. "I like you, Mike. Keep me in the loop. But no more sneaking around here, huh?"

"You have my word," I said.

We shook on it.


S ophie wasn't there when I got back to the Sloth. I texted her and she texted me that she'd be back soon. I took advantage of the down time and sat by the motel pool reading some more Aquinas on my phone.

That's a strange thing to contemplate—the *Summa Theologica* on an electronic device you hold in your hand. Thomas didn't even have the printing press. He wrote the whole thing on parchments with a series of quills. He tilted the entirety of Western thought scribbling at a monk's desk. He believed reason was a gift of God enabling us to find our way to the good and the true. But who uses reason anymore when we have Grok do our thinking for us?

Before I got sucked into the slough of despond, Sophie came back. She parked near the gate, saw me, came in. She gave me a kiss that set the natural rhythms of the Earth on their proper course, then sat on the chaise lounge next to mine.

"I have some things to tell you," she said.

"And I you," I said.

"Who's first?"

"Flip you for it."

"I don't have a coin," she said.

"Fine. Think of a number from one to a hundred."

"What?"

"Go ahead."

She rolled her eyes. "Thirty-seven."

"Wrong. You go first."

"How fair of you," she said with a smile. "So I got in with the protest and made the acquaintance of a couple of students. Talked about the issues, me asking questions, and they were more than happy to fill me in. After a while I made mention of the bombing and asked what they thought about it. They both said they thought it was a terrible thing, not good for their side. One of them said she knew why Eddie did it."

"Do tell," I said.

"He was trying to impress a girl," she said.

"You nailed it."

"Don't sound so surprised."

"Impressed," I said.

"That's not all," Sophie said. "The girl in question, according to this student, is Danica Rendell."

"Mother of pearl," I said. "Motive. The prosecution will find that out. Unless…"

"Unless what?"

"They already have it," I said. "I'm thinking whoever set Eddie up knew about him and Danica."

"You think the prosecutor may be in on this?"

"Probably not," I said. "That would make too many moving parts."

"Your turn," Sophie said. "What did you have to tell me?"

"Nothing important," I said. "A guy tried to kill me with a pitchfork is all."

She closed her eyes. "Talk to me."

I told her about it. When I got to the part where Rendell's legal counsel chewed his nails about a possible lawsuit, my phone buzzed. Local number.

"Romeo," I said.

"This is Detective Gracie. You're the legal rep for Edward Hastings?"

"That's right."

"I'm calling to inform you that your client has confessed."

"What?"

"You need to get down here so we can formalize it."

"Wait a sec—"

The call cut.

"What's going on?" Sophie said.

"We may be heading home sooner than we thought," I said.

I t took me ten minutes to get to the station. I reported to the front desk. The uniform there told me to wait. He came back and had me follow him through a door. We walked past some desks and cubicles. The uniform dropped me off at the last one, where a man sat with his back to us.

"Here he is," the uniform said, and walked on.

The man spun around in his chair. He was around forty, with dusky hair and a neatly trimmed beard. He wore a crisp blue shirt and a tie with purple and turquoise triangles on it.

He stood and said, "I'm Detective Gracie." He didn't extend his hand.

"What's going on?" I said.

"As I told you, your client confessed. To be clear, I didn't question him. No one did. He just started screaming, that he wanted to confess, that he wanted us to know he made the bomb. I told him to be quiet, that he needed to talk to his lawyer before saying anything else. He said he wanted to confess. That's when I called you. But as you know, what he shouted out can be used against him."

"Can I see him now?" I said.

"You understand what I just told you?"

"You made yourself clear," I said.

"This way." He led me through a door to the cell corridor, two on each side. First door on the left was Eddie's.

"I'll check back in ten minutes," Gracie said. "We have a stenographer. We can take the statement and wrap this up."

"A neat little package?"

"Whatever."

He unlocked the door and I went in.

. . .

E ddie was sitting on his bunk, legs up and arms wrapped around his knees.

"What's going on, Eddie?" I said.

"I guess I don't need you anymore," he said.

"Answer my question."

"Why?"

"Humor me."

"Why?"

"Because I've invested a lot of time in you," I said. "I think I deserve an answer."

He rubbed his face. "I'm just tired of the whole thing. I did it."

"Just want to get it off your chest, huh?"

"Yeah."

"Since it doesn't matter anymore," I said, "just for my records, tell me how you did it."

"Did what?"

"The bomb. How'd you make it?"

He shrugged. "I looked it up."

"Uh-huh. And you went to Bombs R Us and got a kit?"

"I don't have to tell you anything," he said.

"Because you can't," I said. "The bomb was made with C4."

"So?"

"How'd you get it?"

"I'm done talking."

"That's your story? You found out how to get your hands on some C4?"

"That's right."

"There's only one thing wrong with your story," I said. "The bomb wasn't made with C4."

He looked at the wall.

I slapped his arms off his knees. He looked at me like I'd shot him.

"I hate waste," I said. "If you waste your life I'll hate you for it. And I don't want to hate you."

He said nothing. His eyes started to water. I sat on the bunk.

"You want to spend the rest of your life in prison just because Danica Rendell doesn't return your texts?"

That got his attention. "How do you know that?"

"Because I work for you, Sophie and Ira Rosen work for you, we've got skin in the game and you're just giving up like Young Werther."

"Like who?"

"A character in a novel by a German guy named Goethe. About a kid your age who gets obsessed with a girl who rejects him, so he kills himself."

"That's....it?"

"And you want to kill yourself, too."

"I do not!"

"Then give us more time. No more confessing. Don't talk to anybody, don't sign anything. If they try to talk to you insist on your lawyer being present. He's coming up here to meet you. Talk to him before you make any more decisions. You're going to love this man. You're going to trust him. You at least owe him that, considering the gas money it's going to take for him to get here. Okay?"

Eddie stared at the wall.

"I didn't hear you," I said.

He took in a deep breath and let it out. "Okay."

"Give me your hand," I said.

"Huh?"

"Shake my hand."

I held out my paw. Eddie took it, limply.

"Squeeze," I said.

He did.

"This is called giving me your word," I said. "It's a sacred trust. Can you remember that?"

"Yeah."

"Welcome back to the fight," I said.

I gave a rap on the door. Detective Gracie came and opened it. "I've got the steno set up," he said.

"Won't be needing it," I said.

"What do you mean?"

"Let's talk," I said. I gave Eddie a nod and stepped into the hallway. Gracie shut the door.

We went back to Gracie's desk. "Okay," he said. "What's going on."

"My client does not wish to confess."

"He already has," Gracie said.

"He was distressed," I said.

"Oh, sure."

"He didn't mean it," I said. "I'm sure you've said things in your life you didn't mean."

"You're really gonna take this to trial?"

"It's in the Constitution," I said.

He shook his head. "Knock yourself out."

No more words passed between us. He took me to the door to the lobby, let me out, and closed the door.

I stood there for a moment. The desk officer gave me a passing look, then went back to his monitor. Just as I got to the front door an officer came in. None other than Mark Jacobsen. His whole body stiffened, like a Greek casting an accidental glance at Medusa.

"We have to stop meeting like this," I said. "People will talk."

He wanted to say something, but walked on past me

without a word. He took a couple of steps and slapped his sidearm.

Subtle this cop was not.

Back at the motel I called Ira and put it on speaker so Sophie could listen. I had a lot to tell him. He only said "Hoo boy" twice during my summary, which I considered a small victory.

We talked about Eddie's upcoming prelim and made plans for Ira's arrival. I told him I could get him a ground floor room at the Somber Sloth, with a view of the swimming pool. He thanked me, though not profusely.

After the call Sophie asked me about Eddie. Did I think he could hold on?

"A slim chance," I said.

"Better than no chance," Sophie said.

I smiled. "You took a chance on me and look what happened."

She put her hand on my cheek. "A good bet, I say."

Next morning Sophie and I had breakfast at Gussie's. Maria was there, glad to see me and meet my wife. I asked about her dad and she said he was getting along as well as could be expected.

Back at the motel, Sophie needed to do some work on lesson plans. I used the time to pay a visit to Grover Hawthorne at the McCracken law office.

The receptionist gave me a pleasant but suspicious smile.

"May I help you?" she said.

"I'm here to see Grover Hawthorne."

"Do you have an appointment?"

"Only with destiny," I said.

"Excuse me?"

"He'll want to see me," I said. "Tell him it concerns Danica

Rendell."

She frowned. "May I have your name?"

"Mike Romeo."

"If you'll have a seat, I'll see if he's available."

"Thank you." I went to a chair by the aquarium. The fish seemed perfectly happy swimming around. I put my hand up to the glass and a red-and-yellow fish dashed out of the way. The Romeo touch.

The receptionist spoke low into her handset.

She hung up and said, "Mr. Hawthorne will be with you in a moment."

I nodded.

The moment turned into half an hour. I figured he was sweating me. An old negotiating trick. I stayed cool by contemplating the fish. They were like college students who swim happily about in their own little bubble, content to be encased in glass. I thought about Plato's cave then, where the people could only see shadows, not the light of the world.

A red-and-yellow fish kept flitting by, giving me the side eye. I wondered what he was thinking. They used to say little fish have only a seven-second memory, but now they say the fishies have memory and even some level of cognitive ability —just like college students. The only question is whether they apply it.

Did my aquatic inquisitor wonder if I was friend or foe? A great big fish? Or was he looking at my Hawaiian shirt and pondering the flora? Did he ponder at all? Did he wish to venture outside the glass to explore but suffer certain death?

This is how I pass the time in a waiting room.

F inally, the receptionist came out from behind the desk and said, "Mr. Hawthorne will see you now."

She led me through a door and down a hallway to an

office. She tapped on the door and a voice said, "Come in."

She opened the door and in I went. The door closed behind me.

It was a supremely neat office with a big window overlooking the buildings that made up the modest downtown. Grover Hawthorne was seated behind a glass-top desk, his coat off, his tie firmly knotted at the throat. He looked up from his open laptop.

"What is it you have to say?" he said.

"Nice to meet you, too," I said.

"This isn't a social visit," he said. "What do you want?"

"I have a question for you."

"Make it fast."

"What's your relationship with Danica Rendell?"

"Who?" Cool as a refrigerated carrot.

"The young woman you met with at Casa Medina yesterday."

He paused and put on a cold, expressionless mask. "I had no such meeting."

"You're going with that? Really?"

"Anything else?" Hawthorne said.

"Grover," I said. "May I call you Grover?"

"No."

"The truth will out, Grove. I was there. I saw you."

He leaned back in his chair. "I had no such meeting."

"Ah, I see," I said.

"See what?"

"The clever lawyer. The non-denial denial."

"What are you talking about?"

"It depends on what your definition of 'meeting' is, right?"

His mouth said nothing but his glare said a lot.

I said, "You might say it wasn't a meeting, but a chance encounter. Okay, let's go with that. What did you discuss with Danica Rendell?"

He steepled his fingers in front of him. "First of all, even if what you say happened, which I deny, I don't owe you anything. I don't know who you are or what you're after. Second of all, I don't care."

"I have a feeling you do know and you do care," I said. "You know that I am part of the legal team representing Eddie Hastings."

"You have no idea what I know."

"But I do," I said. "I am a student of human nature, a reader of palms and faces, a seeker of truth, a teller of tales."

"You're a freak."

"I have my moments."

"You're ridiculous," he said. "A puffer and a poser."

"And a pirate and a poet."

"Just get out."

"I must say, Grove, this meeting has been less than enlightening."

He got up, went to the door, opened it. He stepped outside and pointed down the corridor. "That way."


It was almost noon, and the sun was scorching. It matched my mood.

On the way back to the Sloth, I got a call from Mary Lou Overstreet.

"Hello, Mike. I was wondering if we could get together tonight. At my house, for dinner. Bring your lovely wife, of course."

"What brought this on?" I said.

"I'd like to make up for snapping at you yesterday."

"No need for that," I said. "You were right."

"Not so sure about that," she said. "Shall we say seven o'clock?"

"Seven it is."

She gave me the address and clicked off.

I was still in a fine fettle when I got back to the motel. I know that because I grunted in response to Sophie's welcome.

"I'm tired of running into walls," I said. "And I'm tired of *these* walls. If Dante Alighieri was writing today he'd describe Purgatory as this room, locked from the outside."

"Okay, what happened?" Sophie said.

"Nothing," I said. "Which is the point. I want to get out of here. I want the ocean. I want to smell the beach. I wish I'd never broken up that fight."

"No you don't," Sophie said.

I looked at her resolute face.

"This is what you do," she said. "So lean into it."

That melted the ice ball in my chest. I put my arms around her. "I'd rather lean into you."

"Go ahead and lean."

I put my arms around her. "Question. If you had to choose between chicken wings on the roof, or a home cooked meal at Mary Lou Overstreet's house, which would it be?"

"Mary Lou's, of course," she said. "But where will you be?"

"Hilarious," I said.


An hour later I got a call.

"Mr. Romeo?" The voice was soft and low. I couldn't tell if it was a man or a woman.

"Same," I said.

"Someone would like to meet you." It was a smoky, almost seductive voice. Early Lauren Bacall.

"Intriguing," I said. "Who is this?"

"A go-between."

"Uh-huh. How did you get this number?"

"The party is Caleb Crane."

"Even more intriguing," I said.

"There's an airport out at the end of Milpas Road," the voice said. "Be there in exactly one hour. And come alone."

"If you'll pardon me, this sounds a bit too much like a setup."

"I understand. I assure you the intent is honorable. It's a sunny day and there are other people around. I will meet you inside the terminal. I will be alone."

"My skepticism is still kicking in," I said.

"The choice is yours. One hour."

The call ended.

"So what was that all about?" Sophie said.

"Apparently I'm invited to meet the elusive Caleb Crane."

"Whoa!"

"I better jump in the shower," I said. "I've got one hour."

"Am I coming?"

"The fellow said I'm to come alone. But maybe I can get a selfie with him. Would you like that?"

"I'll pass," she said.

"I'm glad," I said.

The airport had three hangars, a boxy terminal and a control tower that looked like it was built in the fifties. I parked in the small lot and went inside the terminal. There was a lone desk with a couple of guys in white short-sleeved shirts pecking away at keyboards. I was the only other one in there.

I was about to go up to the desk when a voice behind me said, "Mr. Romeo?"

It was a woman, maybe thirty, dressed in a blue business suit. She had short brown hair and wore a surgical mask.

"That would be me," I said.

"My name is Rose." It was that smoky voice. "I arranged this meeting."

"You arrange for Caleb Crane?" I said.

"I help in many ways," she said. "Would you like to come this way?"

She put out her hand as a gesture. The hand and wrist looked a bit thick to me, meatier than I would have anticipated.

We went down a corridor, at the end of which was a set of double doors watched over by a well-fed security guard.

Rose said, "He's with me."

The unsmiling guard got up and grabbed a security wand from a podium.

"Hands out to the side," he said.

I complied. He gave me a wanding. Then he tilted his head to indicate we could move on.

We went through the doors and out to the tarmac, just as a single-engine Cessna taxied to the runway, revved up, and took off.

That was it for activity.

Rose said, "You'll enjoy this. Something you don't see very often."

"I don't see anything," I said.

"Just wait. Caleb is very precise with his timing. It's one of the things that sets him apart."

"What are some other things?"

"You'll find out very soon," Rose said. "In fact..." She pointed to the sky.

It came out of the clouds like some sort of mythical creature from Olympus. Closer and closer, until I could see it was a private jet. A beauty, too, with a wingspan of at least a hundred feet. It made a perfect landing, like a swan on a lake, and taxied to a spot in front of one of the hangars. The door opened and steps lowered.

"Now that's an entrance," I said.

"The best is yet to come," Rose said.

. . .

I followed Rose to the stairs. She indicated I could go up first. So I went. At the top I was met by a chiseled fellow bursting with steroidal muscles. He also wore a surgical mask. He held one out for me.

"No thanks," I said.

He kept it there and told me with his eyes I'd better take it.

Rose was behind me. "Mr. Crane requests that all aboard wear a mask."

"That's fine," I said. "Request denied."

A vein throbbed on the big guy's forehead.

Rose's demeanor and voice stayed calm. "Then you wish to cancel this meeting?"

"I'm not the one who called it," I said.

She nodded. "One moment, please." Off she went.

The big guy stood between me and any further ingress. He gave me a full-on, prison yard glare.

"Having a nice day?" I said.

His eyes did not change.

"How 'bout those Dodgers?"

Glare.

"Do you view ontology as a branch of metaphysics or epistemology?"

The vein in his head engorged. He wanted to rip my lungs out, but something held him back.

I saw no use in further conversation.

Then Rose came back. "If you'll follow me."


The cabin had eight plush seats, recessed lighting, and four monitors, two on each side. The seats were positioned in two sections of four. Two seats faced two in each section.

Rose had me sit in a chair facing aft, on the aisle side.

"May I get you something to drink?" she asked. "We have coffee, but not just any coffee. Kopi luwak."

"Who is Kopi Luwak?"

"Not who, Mr. Romeo. It's the rarest and best coffee in the world. Enjoy it. Just don't ask how it is made."

"How is it made?"

A chuckle from behind the mask. "Are you familiar with the Asian palm civet?"

"Civets are little nocturnal animals."

"Yes, and these are in Southeast Asia. They are fed coffee cherries which ferment in their intestines. When they defecate, the beans are separated and cleaned for grinding and roasting."

"You're serious?"

"Yes, I am."

"So in effect we're drinking poop?"

"Okay, you can joke about it," she said. "But you'll be missing out."

"You know what? You've sparked the spirit of adventure in me. Sure, give me a jolt."

"Be right back," she said.

For a second I thought I was in a movie where the bad guys slip me a drug in a mug of coffee and I wake up strapped to a table in a brightly lit room.

Rose returned and placed a napkin on the burnished African-mahogany table between the seats, and set a mug of coffee on the napkin.

"Don't even think of adding anything to it," Rose said.

She waited expectantly.

I gave it a sip. My taste buds appreciated that.

"Nice," I said. "Earthy, yet smooth. Coaxing, without being strident."

"Really?"

"What Marlow might have sipped on his way to see Kurtz."

"I'm afraid I don't know what you mean."

"I get that a lot," I said. "It's reference to a book by Joseph Conrad called Heart of Darkness."

"What's it about?" Rose asked.

"About a fellow named Marlow who goes to find a fellow named Kurtz deep in the African jungle. Kurtz was a brilliant, charismatic genius in the ivory trade, but hasn't been heard from in a while. Marlow finds him drunk with madness, greed, and cruelty. He's made the natives worship him like a god. They fear him. He displays human heads on stakes, so that might have something to do with it."

"Ew."

"The book is a warning about our own hearts of darkness driving us mad."

Rose blinked a couple of times. "You got all that from the coffee?"

"In just one sip."

She shook her head. "You're an interesting guy. I think you'll find Mr. Crane just as interesting. Good luck."

Luck? An odd word choice. But then I realized I really had hit on something. I was Marlow. I about to meet Kurtz.


I was alone for several minutes. A door opened, and he was there.

Crane was trim and lean-muscled. He was dressed in power casual—turtleneck, gray sport coat and pants, and suede brogues. He could have stepped out of a cover for GQ, but for one thing—he wore a clear plastic face shield. His most prominent feature was curved, predatory nose that would have made an eagle proud.

"So you're Mike Romeo," he said. His smile seemed almost genuine.

I put out my hand to shake. He put his hands up.

"If you don't mind," he said.

"You're a careful one," I said.

"Have to be. You like the coffee?"

"It's earthy, yet…Yes, it's very good."

"Very good for the brain," he said. He sat in the facing leather chair, and crossed his legs.

"You know what my life goal is? I am going to live to be a hundred and forty."

"Wow," I said. "Ambitious."

"Don't you think that's an awesome goal?"

"It's a bit hard to picture," I said.

"I take 78 supplements a day, have a wheat grass cocktail for breakfast which includes spirulina, chlorella, beet root, peppermint leaves and Tahitian breadfruit extract. Think about that. A hundred and forty!"

"Longevity is one thing," I said. "Quality is another."

"And how do you define quality?"

"Quality cannot be defined," I said. "It can only be recognized."

"What do you mean?"

"If you look at a Rembrandt, you see quality. If you look at a crucifix in a jar of urine, you see garbage, unless you've let your mind and conscience atrophy."

He blinked a couple of times. "Look, I don't know where you're coming from with that. Don't try to weird me out."

"I thought we were having a pleasant conversation about quality and life."

"You want to know quality?" he said. "Look at this!"

He made a grand gesture to the interior of the jet.

"Quaint," I said.

"You know what it cost me? Two hundred and sixty mil."

"Aren't you an environment guy?" I said. "You think $CO_2$ is killing us."

"What are you asking that for?"

"Well, if you're concerned about greenhouse gasses and the ozone layer, aren't you dumping a lot of it when you fly this thing?"

Crane smiled. "Friend, my presence is important to the overall, and there's a minimal cost to it."

"Some might call that hypocrisy," I said.

His face became a sheet of ice. "Some people are called upon to lead extraordinary lives, no matter the cost."

"Napoleon thought that," I said. "So did a German loud-mouth with a Charlie Chaplin mustache."

He stiffened. "That's kind of insulting."

"Just an analogy," I said. "We have to know history to keep from repeating it."

"Look, man, look! Meat is bad. Bad for everybody."

"But you yourself are made out of meat."

"This isn't funny. You don't know what you're talking about. And that's why I'm here, my friend. This is my moment, I own it, and I'm the one who can make it happen for everybody, wake everybody up. Don't you want to be awake?"

I was sure awake now. "You have more money than Croe-sus, and—"

"Wait, who?"

"There's an old saying—rich as Croesus. He was an ancient king who was the first to make coins out of gold and silver and was a favorite of the god Apollo."

Crane's eyes widened with awe and wonder. "I like that."

"But he got schooled by a wise man named Solon, who told him happiness never comes from wealth, but from a good life, a good family, and a heroic death."

"Okay, you lost me," Crane said. "What if my money gives me the power to make people happier?"

"*Make* people happier?"

For some reason this brought a huge smile to his face. His eyes went wide, as if he was seeing the heavens open.

"Suppose," he said, "something was bad for people, but that badness could be taken away, without harm. That would make more good, right?"

"Pretty general statement," I said. "You need to give me an example."

"Okay, buckle up," he said. "If, and just accept this for a second, if eating meat is bad, and I could make a way for people not to want to eat meat, that would be good, right?"

I started to say something. He cut me off.

"Just listen. There's a tick, the lone star tick, that spreads something called alpha-gal syndrome. But the only thing AGS does is give people a red meat allergy. That's all, nothing else. So what if I could bioengineer lone star ticks with a greater capacity to spread AGS? Better health, better world!"

After a pause to let the chill in my spine run out, I said, "You're talking about creating a bio-weapon in a lab and unleashing it on the world. China already did that, and how'd that work out? It's a Faucian bargain."

"A what?"

"Sorry, that was a Freudian slip."

"A what?"

"I meant to say Faustian bargain. Essentially, a deal with the devil."

"You shouldn't say that."

"I'm just trying to make you happier."

He gave me a frozen stare for a good five seconds. Then it melted into a smile and dancing eyes.

"You are something else," he said. "I like you. I really do. You really are something."

"Beats being nothing," I said.

"Exactly! You know, you look great. I mean, solid. What do you bench?"

"I don't push weights," I said.

"How do you get those arms?"

"Why don't you tell me——"

"Would you flex for me?" he said.

"Excuse me?"

"Flex. Take off that lovely Hawaiian shirt and flex."

"For this I came out here?" I said.

"How would you like to work for me? As my bodyguard."

"I've already got a job."

"At what pay?"

"That's filed under business, none of yours."

"Is it twenty grand a month? Because that's what I'll start you at. You could buy a lot of shirts. Plus, you'll get to ride around in this."

"Somehow, I don't think I'd be happy in my work."

"I could make you happy." He leaned forward, put his elbows on his knees and rested his chin on his hands. "And you could make me happy."

Stay cool, Romeo. "I'm happy now."

"You have no idea," Crane said. "Why not give it a try?"

"Aristotle once said that one day does not make a summer, nor does a short time make a man blessed or happy."

Crane leaned back. "Yeah, you really are something. Okay, listen. Word is you think I might have some connection to what's going on around here. I'll tell you this much. I've thought about the land here, but I've got deals going all over the place. I don't have time to haggle. And I'm not interested in Rendell Ranch."

"That's what you've got a law firm for," I said. "The McCracken firm."

He shook his head. "I have counsel in L.A. and New York. Nothing here."

"But you do know Baldwin Fish."

"I know lots of people, in and out of politics."

"You've also got a lot of fans out here," I said. "Some say rabid followers."

"I can't control that," he said. "It goes along with all I've accomplished. I'm pretty awesome."

"And certainly not shy."

"What good does that do anybody?" He slapped his knees and stood. "Well, I've said everything I wanted to say. I'd appreciate if you'd leave me out of your musings from here on. And I will leave you out of mine, although…"

"Yes?"

"If you ever want to work for me, I'm leaving the offer open, if you know what I mean."

"I do," I said. "And the answer is still no."

His face went blank, like a robot that had finished its recorded message.

"Rose will see you out." He turned and went out the way he'd come in.

I sat there for a minute pondering the word hubris. The Greeks warned about men with power who began to think themselves the equal of the gods. And paid for it. Prometheus chained to a rock and getting his liver pecked out by an eagle, then growing another liver each day for a fresh pecking, on through eternity. Icarus flying too close to the sun in a private jet made of wax and feathers. Napoleon invading Russia. Brezhnev invading Afghanistan.

Rose snapped me from my ponderings. "This way, Mr. Romeo."

I followed her past the big guy with the forehead vein who was twitching with desire to remove my head.

At the bottom of the stairs Rose said, "I hope you know what a privilege you've had."

"The coffee was amazing," I said. "Do I get a complimentary mug?"

"Goodbye, Mr. Romeo."

. . .

"How'd it go?" Sophie asked. She was sitting on the bed with her laptop.

I plopped next to her. "Will you still love me even if I never get you a private jet?"

"Let me think about it."

She closed her laptop.

"Okay, I've thought about it," she said. "Yes. Now tell me why you asked."

"Caleb Crane has one," I said. "It's a beauty."

"And what would you do with a private jet? Where would you keep it?"

"At the beach," I said. "We could live in it. It's bigger than our mobile."

"That wouldn't be conspicuous at all."

"The very point of having a private jet is to be conspicuous."

"Which is something you don't need to be more of," Sophie said. "So what's he like?"

"Nero," I said. "Too much money, too much power, godlike pretensions."

"Godlike?"

"He wants to live to be a hundred and forty," I said. "Then move to a retirement community in Valhalla."

"What did he want with you?"

"He wanted me to try poop coffee," I said.

"What?"

"He wanted to impress me with his magnificence."

"I'm stuck on the poop coffee," she said.

"I'll explain later," I said. "He wanted me to think he has nothing to do with anything. He also offered me a job."

"What kind of job?"

"Bodyguard with benefits."

She paused. "Does that mean what I think it means?"

"It does," I said. "And he wants me to think he has no interest in Rendell Ranch, no connection with Baldwin Fish or the McCracken law firm."

"Do you believe him?"

"He could be the one pulling the strings, or he could be nothing more than your average, health-obsessed multi-billionaire chucklehead."

"What now, my love?" Sophie said.

"Oh, say that again."

She touched my lips. "Heard melodies are sweet, but those unheard are sweeter."

I took her hand and kissed it. "I just love it when you quote Keats."


Mary Lou Overstreet's house was on a small hill, up a gravel road from the main highway. A smattering of oak trees, *quercus lobata*, surrounded the property. The house itself was a ranch-style design. The front door had a silver knocker shaped like a horseshoe.

"May I?" Sophie said.

"By all means," I said.

She gave the knocker a couple of raps.

A moment later the door opened.

"Welcome to my abode," Mary Lou said. She was wearing a white blouse with pearl buttons, matching slacks, a blazer of whiskey brown, and oxblood ankle boots. "Please come in."

It was a nicely appointed home with a southwest flavor, hardwood floors and flat ceiling with wood beams. She showed us to the living room. It had a stone fireplace over which hung a large painting of cowboys on a cattle drive. On an end table by the sofa sat a cast iron statuette, a longhorn steer the size of a chihuahua.

Through French doors I could see a lighted patio. A man in

a chef's outfit was tending a barbecue pit the size of a Humvee.

"You have a lovely home," Sophie said.

"Thank you," Mary Lou said. "Please make yourselves at home. We're having T-bone steaks tonight and a robust Alto Nova cab from Paso Robles. May I offer you a glass?"

"Please," Sophie said.

"By all means," I said.

We sat on the sofa as Mary Lou went to get the wine.

Sophie reached out and touched one of the horns on the statuette. "Do you think you would have made a good cowboy?"

I thought about it. "Well, I drive Ira crazy. I could drive cattle no problem."

"That's quite a stretch," Sophie said.

"And that would be my name," I said. "Stretch Romeo, fastest gun west of the Pecos."

"Son of a gun, maybe."

"And you could be my saloon gal."

"No," she said. "I'd be the spunky store owner who tames Stretch Romeo."

"Distinct possibility," I said.

Mary Lou returned with a tray with three glasses and the bottle of wine. She set it down on the burnished wood coffee table and expertly wielded a corkscrew to open the bottle. She poured a little in a glass and handed it to me.

I swirled the glass like I knew what I was doing, gave it a sniff, then tasted.

"Well?" Mary Lou said.

I nodded. "Conversational without being verbose."

Sophie face-palmed.

"Flirtatious without being coy," I said.

"You can stop now," Sophie said.

"You missed your calling," Mary Lou said, and poured us

all a glass. She held hers out.

"To new friends," she said.

We clinked and sipped.

Mary Lou sat in a plush leather chair. "How did you two meet?"

Sophie looked at me.

"You go ahead," I said.

Sophie said, "I was working in a bookstore in L.A. when a Hawaiian shirt walked in with him in it."

Mary Lou laughed.

"He bought some books," Sophie said. "But left them at an ice cream store."

"There was a reason for that," I said, not going into the details since they included two guys with guns.

"A friend at the ice cream store brought me the books," Sophie said. "Mike left his address with me for our mailing list. So I walked them over."

"She had me at 'You forgot your books,'" I said.

"I love it," Mary Lou said. "And I—" The doorbell rang.

Frowning, Mary Lou said, "Excuse me."

She put her glass down and went to answer the door.

A few moments later we heard some talking, which got louder.

Mary Lou said, "It's just rude."

A man's voice said, "That's not like you at all."

Mary Lou came back. Behind her was Baldwin Fish.

"Unwanted guest," Mary Lou said.

Fish smiled. "Not at all." He was dressed in gray slacks and blazer, with a white shirt open at the collar. He held a bottle of wine.

"I won't stay long," he said. "Unless Mary Lou invites me to dinner."

"Ha, ha," said Mary Lou.

Fish put the bottle of wine on the coffee table. "Duckhorn

Cabernet. I just wanted to show you and your guests that I'm not the awful caricature you think I am."

"How did you know I was having guests?" Mary Lou said.

"These things float around," Baldwin Fish said. "I would have called, but you know how I like to make an entrance."

With a resigned look, Mary Lou said, "All right, Baldwin. You can have a glass of the Alta Nova, but then you and your wine can go."

Mary Lou went to get another glass. Fish sat himself across from us.

"She really likes me," Fish said.

"That's quite obvious," I said.

"I mean it. She knows deep down I'm a friend of Rendell Ranch."

"That so?"

"We're all on the same team here," Fish said. "I want you to know that. And I want to tell you that anything I can do to find the truth, I'll do it."

"You believe in the truth, do you?" I said.

"I do," Fish said. "You do, too, I'm sure."

"It's why I didn't go into politics," I said.

Sophie shook her head.

Fish laughed. A politician's laugh—not overly exuberant, but just enough to identify with the common man. Of which I was apparently one.

"We're not all cut from that cloth," Fish said.

"What cloth is that?" Mary Lou said, coming back in with a wine glass. She put it on the table in front of Fish.

"I was just telling these fine folks that I'm not your typical politician," Fish said. He reached for the open bottle and poured some in his glass.

"Oh, really?" Mary Lou said.

"Because I tell the truth," Fish said.

"Right," Mary Lou said, drawing out the word.

Fish turned to me. "Do you hear that? This is the respect I get?"

Sophie shifted uncomfortably next to me.

Baldwin Fish said, "To your health," and sipped his wine.

"What is the real reason you're here, Baldwin?" Mary Lou said.

He put his glass on the table. "There is a reason." He reached inside his coat and pulled out a tri-folded piece of paper. He opened it and handed it to Mary Lou.

We all watched her read it. And watched her eyes enflame.

"Who sent this?" she said.

"Anonymous," Fish said.

"So what good is it?"

"Maybe if you ask me to stay, I can tell you."

"Don't be juvenile," Mary Lou said.

"May I see that?" I said.

Mary Lou handed me the paper. It was an email to Baldwin Fish. The entire message was: *More cows will die. Only you can stop it.*

Fish said, "I showed this to my computer guy, sharp kid. He was able to trace the sending IP to the Drake College library."

"Unbelievable," Mary Lou said. "Can we find out who it was?"

"Maybe," Fish said. "The time stamp says 11:42 a.m."

"Students usually have to log in with a student ID," I said.

"Right," Fish said.

"But a fake ID is not out of the question."

Mary Lou cursed, then said, "Excuse me."

"The library should have security cameras," I asked.

"Yes," Fish said. "We can look at the footage."

"Not without a subpoena," I said.

"How's that?" Fish said.

"You'll need a subpoena duces tecum," I said. "To compel

the production of documents and records, including security footage. The library can push back, and the whole thing get tangled up in court."

"Well, this is a fine way to start a dinner party," Mary Lou said. "All right, Baldwin, you can stay. I'll have Rudolfo throw on another steak."

A nd so we dined.
Well, three of us mostly dined. Baldwin Fish mostly talked.

He talked about his "vision" for California, a "transformation" where people could come together once again in the "Golden State."

He talked about his father coming to California to practice law, later becoming a judge. And his mother who was active in local politics, and that "everybody loved her."

"That's the example I'd like to follow," he said.

I couldn't contain myself. "You want everybody to love you?"

"Isn't that a worthy goal?"

"For a cinnamon bun maker," I said. "But not for a politician."

"Why do you say that, Mr. Romeo?" He leaned forward as if he were interested.

"Civil government is not there to be loved," I said. "It's there to be respected and sometimes feared."

"Feared?" Fish said. "That sounds like fascism."

"Or the rule of law," I said. "Do we want murderers to love the government or fear it?"

"All right, boys," Mary Lou said.

"No, let's hear him out," Fish said.

Mary Lou said, "Baldwin, dear, draw in your tail feathers."

He shot her a look. "I didn't come here to be insulted."

"You weren't invited, either," Mary Lou said.

Fish started to say something, then covered it up with a smile.

"Quite right," he said. "I apologize to all." He raised his wine glass to us, then drained it.

D essert was key lime pie.
        After dinner, Mary Lou served brandy in the living room.

Sophie and I sipped ours with genteel restraint. Fish swigged his.

"Better slow down, Baldwin," Mary Lou said. "You might say something you'll regret."

"I'll say something right now," Fish said. "Rendell Ranch needs to get off its a… I mean, accept the future."

"Oh, Baldwin," Mary Lou said.

"You know it and I know it," Fish said.

"I don't know anything of the kind," Mary Lou said.

"Well, you should." Fish drank more brandy.

"Shall we change the subject?" Mary Lou said.

"What are you afraid of?" Fish said, almost snarling.

"Please be quiet," Mary Lou said.

"Maybe it's time for us to go," I said.

"Stick around," Fish said. "Or you may miss the best part."

"Mr. Fish," I said, "the Good Book says wine is a mocker and beer a brawler. I think that makes brandy a boxer with an iron fist."

"What are you even talking about?" Fish said.

"Say, how about those Dodgers?" Sophie said. "They're the team to beat, aren't they?"

Mary Lou cracked up.

Baldwin Fish scowled, sat back in his chair, and drank more brandy.

Which made the timing perfect for the text sent to my phone. It was from Jamie Anderson. Asking if I could meet him at the park. Urgent.

"It looks like we really do have to go," I said, standing. "Mary Lou, thank you for an enjoyable evening."

"It's not ending like I wanted it to," Mary Lou said.

"Come on," Fish said. "Stay. I'm sorry."

"Have some coffee," I said.

Sophie shook Mary Lou's hand. "Thank you for the dinner. It was nice meeting you, Mr. Fish."

Fish lifted his glass to her.

In the car, Sophie said, "That was truly weird."

"Or completely normal," I said.

"How so?"

"A politician who drinks to excess? It's almost a cliché. Some use it, some are used by it. I peg Baldwin Fish as the second kind."

Sophie nodded. "Maybe he'll be the source of a new cliché."

"How's that?" I said.

"People will say he drinks like a Baldwin Fish."

"I'm glad I married you," I said.


Only a sliver of moon offered soft luminescence at the park. I took us to the same bench where I'd met with Jamie before, and there he was.

"Thanks for coming," he said.

We sat on the bench.

"We're relieved," I said. "You rescued us from the company of one Baldwin Fish."

"You were with him?" Jamie said.

"At Mary Lou Overstreet's house. He was an uninvited dinner guest."

"Perfect," Jamie said. "That's why I called this little meeting."

"Talk to me," I said.

"I think Bill Peale was working on a story about Fish. I'm not entirely sure. He would have kept it on the down low, even with me. He was careful that way. If I could just find his notes."

"Have you checked his house?" I said.

"I don't have a key," Jamie said.

"One doesn't always need a key."

"You mean, break in?"

I shook my head. "The art of the picked lock is not lost on me."

"Very cool," Jamie said. "Let's try—"

*Bam.*

Jaime doubled over. I knew he'd been shot, and the general direction from which it had come.

I put my arms around Jamie and Sophie and pulled us off the bench, flat on the ground.

Another shot. It hit the bench.

I said, "Sophie, crawl under the bench."

She did.

"Jamie, how bad?" I said.

"My leg, lower leg."

"Can you move?"

"I don't know."

"Hang on."

I took his arm and put it around my neck. Staying low, I dragged him behind the bench.

Another shot hit wood.

The dirt lot where Spinoza sat was twenty yards away.

Not many choices when one guy is wounded, your wife is there, you've got no weapon and little cover. Trying to get them to the car was out.

"Stay down," I said. I pushed up and ran, bent over, to Spinoza.

Another shot cracked.

I opened my trunk and threw back the carpet and got the 9mm I'd taken off a gangbanger some time back.

The magazine was stuffed. I pulled the slide and chambered a round.

Somewhere, a woman screamed.

I ran back to the bench, knelt.

"He's bleeding pretty bad," Sophie said. "Here."

She guided my hand to Jamie's calf. His pants were wet with blood.

I put the gun down, took off my shirt and wrapped it around the wound. There was enough of it to make an overhand loop and pull tight.

"We've got to get you to emergency," I said. "Where is it?"

"Maybe five miles," Jamie said.

"Sophie, stay low and get to Spinoza."

"Who's Spinoza?" Jamie said.

"Go, Sophie."

She took off. I picked up my gun and put it in the back of my waistband.

"Put your arm around my neck," I said. I got Jamie to his feet. He cried out in pain.

"Piggyback time," I said. "Hang on."

I crouched, grabbed both his arms by the wrists, and hoisted him. Then ran for the car.

No more shots fired. Could be good or bad. It could be the guy took off after I fired off my rounds. Or it could mean he was making his way closer.

And what was the woman screaming about?

I put Jamie in the front seat, gave the keys to Sophie.

"Drive him there. Call me when you're inside."

"You're staying?"

"I want to see if that woman's okay."

"Mike, I'm sure—"

"Go on," I said. "Now."

As she drove off, I realized I had a bit of a problem. I was a shirtless guy wandering around a park with an illegal handgun. Not exactly inconspicuous.

I got to a tree and stood there, looking and listening, trying to see if anything was moving, or if I could hear more signs of distress. All was silence and shadows.

The lights of a passing car briefly lit up my spot. I circled around the tree to avoid the lights, like a squirrel being chased by a dog.

In the dim I saw a wire trash bin next to a cement picnic table.

The car passed and I waited. Still no sign of movement, no noise except the ambient sound of cars from the street on the other side of the park.

I went to the trash bin and used my phone to illuminate the contents. A plastic Topo Chico bottle was on top of a couple crumpled white bags, with a half-eaten top of a bun off to the side.

I pulled one of the bags. It was from Chick-fil-A. I opened it and dumped out two wadded-up napkins and a depleted ketchup packet.

I put my gun in the bag and curled it closed.

Then I went to look for the woman, having no idea if the shooter was still around. Maybe the woman was with him, or taken by him, or hurt by him. Or maybe there was no connection at all. My thoughts were as jumbled as the trash in the basket.

I kept to the perimeter of the park and used trees as stopping points. This got me closer to the busier street, with more cars and more lights. At least the lights gave me a better look at this part of the park. I saw no people, no movements. My sense was whoever had screamed was gone now. So, too, the shooter.

I was limited in what I could do. Waiting to hear from Sophie while keeping out of sight was probably best.

But the best laid plans of mice and men often go awry, as Bobby Burns told us.

A spotlight hit me and a loudspeaker voice said, "Put your hands on your head and don't move."

J ust do what the cops tell you to do. How many disastrous encounters could have been avoided if the subject of inquiry just kept his yap shut and did what he was told?

I dropped the bag with the gun on the ground and put my hands on my head.

The cop car kept the spot on me as two officers approached. One was tall and the other short, like some old-time Vaudeville comedy team. They had their hands poised over their sidearms.

"You mind telling us what you're doing?" the tall one said.

"Not at all," I said. "Can I put my hands down?"

"No, sir."

"That means you're detaining me, but you don't have reasonable suspicion."

Pause. "There was a report about shots fired," Officer Tall said.

"I can explain all that," I said. "I was the one who got shot at."

"All right," Officer Tall said. "You can put your hands down. What's going on?"

"My name is Mike Romeo. I work for a lawyer. We're representing Eddie Hastings in the newspaper bombing case. I came here for a meeting with a reporter named Jamie Anderson. My wife was with me. We were sitting on a bench. There was a shot, I'm sure it was a rifle, and Jamie was hit in the leg. Another shot fired hit the bench. You can check that out. We managed to get to my car. I had my wife drive Jamie to the hospital. That's it so far."

Another pause. "Why aren't you wearing a shirt?" Tall asked.

"I had to use it to bind Jamie's wound," I said. "You can check that, too."

"You have some ID?"

"Yes. May I get it for you?"

"Go ahead."

I reached slowly into my front pocket and took out my wallet. I took out my driver's license and one of Ira's cards. I held them out. Officer Short got into the action by stepping up and taking them.

The two looked at the items with a flashlight.

"Okay," Officer Tall said.

Officer Short handed them back to me.

"Another thing," I said. "I heard a woman scream after one of the shots. I tried to locate her, but couldn't't."

"She may have been the one to call in the report," Officer Tall said.

"Try to find her," I said. "She may have seen the shooter."

"What are you going to do now?" Tall asked.

"Wait for my wife to call and have her come pick me up."

Tall said. "How about we drive you there? We can talk to the victim."

"I don't mind waiting," I said.

"I think it would be better if you came with us."

"Can I bring my dinner?" I pointed to the bag.

"Of course," Officer Tall said.

W hen you're in the back of a police vehicle, with two officers in front, having an illegal firearm on your lap can be a bit nerve wracking.

So when Officer Short said I could eat if I wanted to, I said, "My tummy's a little sketchy right now. I think I'll wait."

"I hear you," Short said.

Tall said, "We get that way every night on patrol."

The two officers laughed.

"So you're from L.A.?" Short said.

"Does it show?"

"I have a friend with LAPD. He wants out. He wants to get up here."

"I don't blame him," I said.

"He was on the street during the riots. He got hit with a chunk of concrete."

"From a mostly peaceful protestor," I said.

"Yeah, right," Short said. "What was it like to be there?"

"Warm and friendly," I said. "They set cars on fire and roasted marshmallows."

"Funny guy," Tall said.

A t emergency reception the two officers said hello to the desk jockey—a portly guy with thick hair and a dusting of beard—as if they were old friends.

The desk jockey looked at me with barely concealed suspicion.

"He's with us," Officer Tall said. "We want to see Anderson, was just brought in."

Desk Jockey tapped a keyboard, looked at a monitor. Nodded. And buzzed us in.

A nurse stopped walking when she saw us.

"Hey, Juana," Officer Tall said.

"What's going on?" Nurse Juana said.

Tall jerked a thumb at me. "Can we get this guy a robe or something?"

Juana looked at me. "He's a big one. Just a second."

She went to a cabinet and pulled out a folded hospital gown.

"Will this do?" she said.

"I always wanted to start a fashion trend," I said. I took the gown.

Officer Short put out his arm. "I'll hold your bag for you."

"That's okay," I said, quickly opening the gown and putting it on like a shirt, with the ties in front. I put my left arm through, switched the bag from my right hand to my left, then put my right arm through.

Officer Tall said, "Where is Anderson?"

Juana said, "This way."

She led us to a curtained bay. Jamie was sitting up in a bed, his right leg wrapped in gauze. Sophie was standing next to him. She came over to me and took my hand.

"You okay?" she said.

Before I could answer, Officer Tall said, "Mr. Anderson, how're you doing?"

"I guess I'm all right," Jamie said.

"I'm Officer Tanner, and this is Officer Plante. Feel up to telling us what happened?"

"Mike didn't tell you?" Jamie said.

"We'd like to hear it from you, and record it with your permission."

"No problem," Jamie said.

Officer Plante, formerly Small, took out a handheld digital recorder, prepped it, and said, "Ready."

Jamie gave them his account, which matched mine.

When he finished, Officer Tanner said, "We'll submit this and see what we can find out. Our lead officer on cases like this may want to talk to you himself."

"I'm not leaving town," Jamie said.

"And you?" Tanner asked me.

"I'll be here," I said.

Tanner reached in his pocket, pulled out a card and gave it to me. "Anything else comes to you, give me a call."

The law left us.

I said to Jamie, "I want to check out Bill Peale's house."

"Now?" Jamie said.

"Now. Where might he have kept notes?"

"His house has a bedroom he used as an office," Jamie said. "Kind of messy. There's a desk."

"Computer?"

"His laptop, but he carried it back and forth. It got destroyed in the blast."

"Give me the address."

"You're going dressed like that?" Sophie said.

"Would you prefer I go skins?"

She looked at the bag in my hand. "Were you hungry?"

"I'll explain all in due course," I said.

"Exclusive," Jamie said.

Bill Peale's house was on a corner lot. The neighborhood was quiet except for a distant sound of Salsa music. I parked a couple of houses away. I didn't see anybody on the street as I got to the door, my lock pick set in hand.

But I didn't have to pick the lock. The door pushed open. The deadbolt was out, the doorjamb splintered. The front room was dark except for ambient light from another room.

Where a scratching sound came from. Then the sound of something thrown on the floor. I could see the place had been tossed. Sofa pillows scattered, coffee table overturned. A bookshelf was devoid of books, the volumes tossed in haphazard piles on the floor.

Across the room was a fireplace. Next to it was an iron fireplace tool set—-poker, shovel, tongs. I stepped quietly over and removed the poker.

I padded to the adjoining room and took a peek inside.

Somebody was trashing it. Someone I knew.

"Hi, Dante," I said.

He spun around like a caffeinated dervish.

One look at me and he went for something. It was a baseball bat, sitting on the desk.

I pounced as his arm reached the weapon. And my poker rapped his arm.

Dante howled.

I swept the bat off the desk with the poker, dropped it, and twisted Dante's arm behind him.

More howling.

I forced him to his knees. His howl morphed into a wail.

"Shut up," I said.

"Lemme go!"

Still holding his arm I pushed him flat and put my knee on his back. He sucked for air.

"Settle down now," I said. "We need to talk."

"Let go of me, man!"

"In time," I said. "You're going to tell me some things."

He gave me a two-word answer that did not indicate cooperation.

"Don't make this hard," I said.

He spat the same two words, with added emphasis.

"You're going to talk," I said. "Or do you want more pain?"

He chuffed, said nothing.

"You going to talk?" I said.

He told me what I could do to myself, which wasn't nice.

"Have it your way," I said. "Welcome to the inferno, Dante."

I t only took five seconds to loosen his tongue.

"Okay, okay!" he said. "Stop!"

"Do you know what a lie detector is, Dante?"

"Yes!"

"I have one inside me," I said. "It's got wires and paper and squiggly needles, old school. You with me?"

"It hurts!"

I lessened my hold fifty percent.

"Now I'm going to ask you some questions," I said. "And if my squiggly needles start jumping around, well, I'll have to do this."

I ratcheted his arm up.

He screamed.

"We clear on the rules?" I said.

"Yeah, yeah," he said. "Let me go."

"Not yet," I said. "Let's do a test run. What are you looking for here?"

Pause. "Computer stuff."

"What kind of stuff?"

"Whatever. Laptop, hard drives, thumb drives."

"Why?"

"That's what I was told."

"By who?"

"I don't know names."

A needle inside me moved. I spiked his pain.

He screeched. "I swear!"

"On your mother's grave?"

"Yes!"

"Was your mother cremated?"

"Stop, please!"

I let up a little. "We can go on this way all night. I want to know who you're working for."

"Lemme go. I'll tell it straight. I can't think like this!"

"I'll let you sit," I said, releasing him. "Put your back against the desk."

He did.

I picked up the poker. "I can use this in several ways."

"Don't, man."

"Why are you here, Dante?"

"Why else?" He rubbed his shoulder. "Money."

"Who's paying you?"

"I don't know."

I slapped the poker on the floor.

"I swear," he said. "I get bills in my box. A guy calls me on what to do."

"So you have his number?"

"He calls from a burner."

"You aren't the least bit curious who it is?"

"Yeah I am, but I know enough not to ask."

"How'd you get recruited?"

He didn't answer. I patted my palm with the poker.

"Okay," he said. "I get a call one night. Guy says he's been watching me, likes how I handle myself and do I want to make some easy money? And I say yeah, but who's asking? And he says don't ask. Then he says let's try things out, and he says go and spend a day being security for the kids at Drake doing a protest. So I do, and I end up with five hundred in bills. So that's how I get things to do, like tonight."

"Does the name Caleb Crane mean anything to you?"

"I've heard of him," Dante said.

"You're not connected?"

He shook his head. "My arm, man, it's killing me."

"That brings up another question. And I'm only going to ask you once. If I see a flicker of mendacity in your eyes, it's going to be the poker for you."

He frowned. "What's men…"

"Dacity. It means telling a lie. You understand what I'm saying?"

"Oh, man."

"You nervous?"

"Yeah I am!"

"Don't worry," I said. "I'm a good judge. Sure, I make mistakes sometimes. I've broken a few bones that way."

"Aw, come on."

"So you just do your best to be completely truthful with me, yeah?"

I tapped the floor with the poker.

"Yeah, yeah, okay."

I said. "Did you shoot a rifle tonight?"

"Rifle? No way."

I raised the poker.

"I'm tellin' you the truth!"

I rested the iron on my shoulder. "You know what, Dante? I believe you."

He let out a breath of profound relief and dropped his head.

"What did you find here?" I said.

"Nothing," he said.

"Nothing at all?"

He shook his head.

"I'm going to search you, Dante."

"You don't…I don't…"

I raised the poker.

He cursed softly. Then reached in his shirt pocket and took out a couple of thumb drives. He handed them to me.

"What else?" I said.

"That's all," he said. "I swear."

"Mind if I pat you down?" I said.

"Go ahead."

"Good enough," I said. "I have another question."

He looked at me like a man clinging to a vine off a steep cliff.

"Same rules," I said, wagging the poker. "Did you bomb the newspaper office?"

"Whoa whoa whoa. No way! I had nothing to do with that."

"But you know who did," I said.

"No, man, no. I don't know nothin' about that."

"Do you have any idea who it might have been?"

"I don't. Really."

I let him sweat for a moment.

"Dante, you passed my test," I said.

He slumped with relief.

"Now all you have to do is talk to the cops," I said.

"Oh, no no."

"Oh, yes yes."

"They'll kill me," he said.

"Who'll kill you?"

"I don't know! That's just it."

"You've got no choice," I said. "I've got an innocent client."

"No, please, just let me go. I never wanted this."

"We don't want a lot of things in life," I said. "But they happen. So do consequences."

"Listen, I have brother in Bartlesville, Oklahoma. I'll get out of town and go there. I won't come back."

I shook my head. "You've spent many years lying to people, hurting people. You're going to start telling the truth. It'll be good for your soul."

"I don't care about that," he said.

"Start," I said.

I called Officer Tanner.

"You said to call if something came up," I said.

"Yeah," Tanner said.

"It came."

As we waited, Dante told me some of his story. Foster homes. Abuse. Beating up one of his foster dads and leaving him to die. Did a year for that. He wasn't maudlin about it. He told it matter-of-factly. I felt some sympathy for the guy, but not every hard luck kid ends up a thug. He had choices and he made the wrong ones.

Tanner and Plante showed up. I explained the situation. I did not mention the thumb drives. They cuffed Dante and took him away.

I went back to the hospital and told Sophie and Jamie all about my encounter. Jamie wondered if it was Dante who shot him.

"I don't think so," I said. "I gave him a lie detector test."

"Huh?" Jamie said.

"I admit it's a rather personal test," I said. "Not admissible in any court of law, or even any police station, maybe not even a barroom. But I can rely on it."

I took the thumb drives from my pocket. "I got these."

Somebody said, "What've you got?"

It was Detective Gracie, stepping into Jamie's room from the busy hospital corridor.

I closed my hand.

"Open your hand," Gracie said.

"No."

"You want me to arrest you?"

"For what?"

"Withholding evidence," he said.

"You don't have reasonable cause to believe that," I said.

"Just open your hand," he said.

"No."

And we had what is known in the trade as a Mexican standoff, only without weapons.

"There are two witnesses here to observe your behavior," I said. "To search me, you need a warrant based on probable cause, and you clearly don't have that. There are no exigent circumstances, nor is your safety a concern, since this is a brightly lit hospital room with people around. That leaves us with what is called a consensual encounter, which means I don't have to talk to you. So I won't."

Frustration crawled into his eyes. "You're a smart one, aren't you?"

"Am I smart?" I said to Sophie.

"He has his days," she said to Gracie.

Gracie said, "I want to know what happened at the park."

"Your officers took statements," I said.

"Mind if I hear it again?" he said.

"We were at the park," I said. "The three of us and—"

"Why?" Gracie said.

"Just talk."

"About?"

"Detective, that is not relevant. You need me to explain relevance to you?"

Sophie put her hand on my arm.

"We were at the park, on a bench," I said. "Somebody from across the park took a shot us. A rifle. Mr. Anderson was hit. We got him in my car and my wife drove him here. I stayed to try and find the guy."

"That wasn't smart," Gracie said.

"I do the best I can," I said.

"Is that it?"

"I think you have all you need," I said.

"I'll want to talk to you when you get out," Gracie said to Jamie.

To me he said, "Don't get too cute."

That was his exit line.

When he was gone I said to Sophie, "Am I cute?"

"You have your days," she said.

"Mike," Jamie said. "Hand me my wallet. It's in that bag."

A plastic hospital bag was on the over-bed table by the wall. I fished out his wallet and gave it to him. He opened it and took out a folded piece of paper.

"Jess Rendell's address in Fresno," he said.

"You don't rest, do you?" I said.

"Intrepid reporter," he said.

"When you talk to Gracie," I said, "stick to the park. He doesn't need to know about the thumb drives."

"Aren't they evidence?"

"Of what? They're Peale's personal property. Gracie'd have to get a warrant, but he needs more than pure speculation."

"I don't think he likes you," Jamie said.

"Am I unlikable?" I asked Sophie.

"That's enough of that," she said.

At the nurse's station I told the woman to make sure Security was vigilant tonight. She said that was standard with wounds of violence.

Wounds of Violence. Good title for a thriller. Or my biography.

It was almost eleven when we got back to our room. I ditched the hospital gown and put on a T-shirt. I put one of the thumb drives in my computer and double-clicked the icon.

Three folders came up, labeled Vacation Plans, Family Photos, Personal Accounting. Also a few Word docs—

Conspiracies, Historical Mysteries, Bible Prophecy, Geneal-
ogy, Memoir, Novel.

"Let's start with conspiracies," I said.

"Apt," Sophie said.

At the top was written, *Follow the money.* Under that were
a couple of squibs.

New York, 1913. Officially: accidents. Unofficially:
coordinated arson. Tenements, immigrant families—mostly
Italian. Seven fires. Official conclusion: "Poor construction
and carelessness." Weeks after last fire, plots purchased.
Reporter wrote story. "Crime of Profit." A week later his
apartment burned. Official conclusion: "Stove left burning."

Los Angeles, 1952. Officially: suicide. Unofficially:
silenced.

Deputy DA found dead in garage, motor running,
windows up. No note. Working a case on city contracts for
freeway expansion. Displacement of Latino neighborhoods.
Eminent domain. Parcels flipped through dummy buyers.
Reporter tried to follow up. Story killed.

"What do you make of it," Sophie asked.

"He's right about following the money," I said. "That's
usually what these things boil down to."

"A lot of money flew in to visit you today."

"A lot doesn't even begin to describe it."

I opened the Historical Mysteries folder. It held several docs
—Cleopatra's Tomb, Amelia Earhart, Black Dahlia, The
Hinterkaifeck Murders.

"What's that Hinter one?" Sophie said.

I opened it. It had a website link and some text below.

In the small Bavarian farmstead of Hinterkaifeck, Andreas Gruber and his wife lived and tended to their land, along with their daughter and her small children. At the end of March 1922 all six members of the household were found brutally slain with an axe. The crime remains unsolved to this day.

"Dear God," Sophie said.

"Let me try this," I said. I did a global search for *Rendell*. It brought up two hits, both in the Memoir doc.

That night I broke bread with Travis Rendell. Good man. The kind they don't make anymore. Rendell Ranch was booming, and he was pleased with the story I'd written for the Dispatch.

"You ought to write a book," he told me.

"I'll consider it," I said.

And that's the moment I decided to start The Great Unfinished Novel. It's been a rousing success as it remains unfinished to this day.

"Let's try the other drive," I said. I popped it in. Only one folder came up, labeled News_Backup. I double-clicked. A message came up. *The folder Personal_Backup can't be opened because you don't have permission to see its contents.*

"Great," I said.

"Now what?" Sophie said.

"Maybe Jamie knows the password. If not, we turn it over to Ira."

"That seems like a good idea for lots of things."

"Absolutely," I said.

"Another good thing is sleep," Sophie said.

"True that," I said. "With a good night kiss."

"True that," Sophie said.

. . .

I n the morning Sophie needed to do more work for school. I decided to take a field trip.

I drove up the 145 to Fresno. The day was sunny and warm, with puffy clouds in a blue sky. With the top down on Spinoza, I felt like the quintessential Californian before the state got handed over to idiots, where a guy in a Mustang convertible was King of the Road.

Took me a little over an hour to get to the "Raisin Capital of the World." GPS got me to the house ten minutes later. It was a classic Craftsman-style, two-story home, with one of those nice front porches. The front yard had a manicured lawn and some drought-tolerant plants—Agave succulents, Red Yucca, Lavender. The house itself was a warm beige with stone accents.

I parked in front. And heard the sound of an axe splitting wood. It came from the back yard. I let myself in through a side gate.

The back yard was mostly dirt, but looked like it was being prepped for seed or sod. In the middle of the yard was a big tree stump. A man stripped to the waist had his back to me. He picked up a piece of wood from a pile, put it on the stump and gave it a healthy whack with a double-edged axe.

"That's quite a Vargstal you've got there," I said.

The man whipped around. He looked a bit like Travis, had the same body shape. His arms and hands were as solid as concrete.

"What'd you just say?" he said.

"Your axe," I said. "The vikings had a name for a double blade, the Vargstal."

He did not look impressed. "Who are you and what're you doing on my property?"

"Name's Mike. I wonder if I could have a word with you."

"Why?"

"About Rendell Ranch," I said.

He held the axe in both hands, level with the ground. He could swing it in any direction.

"Travis send you?" he said.

"No."

He raised the axe, and for a split second I thought he might throw in at me. But he spun around and thrust it into the stump. It bit hard and stayed.

He turned back to me. Sweat glistened on his face and chest. "You're invading my privacy."

"I know."

"I don't like that."

"Neither do I."

"Then why are you doing it?"

"It's my job," I said. "I work for a lawyer in Los Angeles. We're representing the guy accused of bombing the Central Valley Dispatch."

He gave me a long, hard stare. "What's that got to do with me?"

"I'm just trying to put pieces together," I said. "You're a missing piece."

"You think I had something to do with it?"

"I didn't say that," I said.

"I asked if you think it."

"Not particularly."

"What's that supposed to mean?"

"Means I'm open," I said.

"I don't care what you are," he said. "Get outta here."

"Jess, I've come a long way."

He took a step toward me, told me he didn't give an eff, and that I should get gone before I got hurt.

"You do look like a man who can bring the hurt," I said.

"Don't try to find out," he said.

"Not me," I said. "I prefer civil conversation. That's all I'm asking for."

"You're defending the kid who killed Bill Peale?"

"Accused of," I said. "I don't think he did it."

"Of course you'd say that."

"I believe it, too."

"Bill Peale was a good man," Jess Rendell said. "Why should I help you?"

"Because the real guy is out there walking around."

He thought it over, and looked at me like he was assessing a bull that was up for auction.

"Might as well get out of the sun," he said.

W e went to the back porch and he had me sit in a wooden rocking chair.

"Be right back," he said and went in the house. I rocked and looked at the yard and the stump with the axe in it. I imagined the place with good grass and some flowers along the fence. Zinnias or marigolds maybe. Beauty for its own sake. Put it where you can. I rocked and longed to be back at the beach, on the porch with Sophie, listening to the waves and looking at our petunias.

Jess came back with a tray that held a pitcher, two glasses, and ice bucket, and a bottle of Jack Daniels. He had a shirt on.

He put the tray on a table and sat in the other chair. He put ice in the glasses with tongs, then filled them from the pitcher.

"Lemonade," he said.

He opened the bottle of Jack and held it over my glass. "Have a shot?"

"No thanks," I said.

He handed me the glass, then poured a glug of JD into his glass.

"I call this Rendell Lemonade." He put the bottle down,

took a drink. I did the same.

"This is really good," I said.

"Secret's in the rind," Jess Rendell said. "You rub it around in the pitcher before you add the juice."

"Family recipe?"

"Grandma Addie," Jess said. "She was the daughter of a Texas drover named Gus Walker. She had a gold tooth. And she had stories."

"About cowboys?" I said.

"Real cowboys," Jess said. "Like Teddy Blue Abbott and Ace Harmon."

He smiled at the memory and had another drink. "What's an L.A. lawyer doing mixed up in this thing?"

I told him about my trip to talk to a witness, stopping at Gussie's, about the dinner at Rendell Ranch that Danica interrupted, and some of the rest of the events, including getting shot at.

By the time I finished he'd drained his glass. He poured in more lemonade and Jack.

"That's one whale of a story," he said. "What do you think is going on?"

"I think somebody's after the ranch," I said. "I think Bill Peale was looking into it and they killed him and set up my client as the fall guy."

Jess Rendell thought about it. "You got any idea who could possibly do that?"

"Caleb Crane, maybe."

"That weirdo?"

"He's a weirdo with a lot of money. I met him."

"Crane?"

"On his private jet."

Jess Rendell shook his head. "Too much money. Makes you soft."

"I don't have that problem," I said.

"Bein' soft?"

"Having too much money."

He chortled. "I know that feeling."

I put my empty glass on the table. Jess poured me a refill.

"Jess, I have to ask you this. Are you trying to get the ranch back?"

He stiffened. He looked at me for a full five seconds. "You sayin' you think I had something to do with what happened?"

"I'm not saying that."

"You thinkin' it?"

"No."

"If you were, and I was about twenty years younger, I might punch you in the face."

"I would not want to be punched in the face by you," I said.

"You look like you can handle yourself. You'd give as good as you got." He took a drink. "I don't care about the ranch or my brother."

"Why the bad blood?"

He shrugged. "Old story, I guess. We were different from the get go. Travis was always reading. I was always getting in trouble. I went off to the Marines. Travis went off to college. We both knew ranching, 'cause of our dad. We grew up doing everything. Cleaning stalls, putting up fences, calving, tagging, hauling grain. We both rode, and were always racing each other. Travis liked to win. I hated to lose. That wasn't gonna end good. When I got back from Afghanistan with all my body parts, I was ready to take over the ranch. But Travis was already there, and my dad made his choice. I told him off, I told Travis off, and hopped on a motorcycle and never looked back."

He took a long drink.

"Blood is thicker than Jack Daniels," I said.

"You say some strange things."

"So I've been told."

"What's that say on your arm?"

I told him.

"That's a wacky thing to put on an arm."

"I tend to color outside the lines."

Jess smiled. "Me, too."

I heard a door close inside the house.

"I think you're gonna be interested in this," Jess said.

A moment later the back door swung open and Danica Rendell came out.

"I'm back," she said. Then she saw me and froze.

"It's all right, Danny," Jess said. "This fella might want to ask you a question or two."

Danica said nothing. Her body was tense as fence wire.

"It's okay, honey," Jess said. "Pull up a chair."

She didn't move. For a second I thought she might bolt back into the house. But she did as her uncle requested and pulled a chair next to his. She sat in it slowly, her hands gripping the arms like claws.

"Hi, Danica," I said. "My name's Mike. I work a for a lawyer."

"An L.A. lawyer," Jess said with a smirk.

"We represent Eddie Hastings," I said.

She said nothing.

"Do you know Eddie?" I asked.

She nodded.

"How well?" I asked.

Danica looked at Jess, like she wanted him to run interference for her.

He put his hand on her arm. "Just tell him what you know, and if you don't know anything, that's okay."

She put her hands on her lap, took a deep breath and said,

"He's kind of been after me to go out with him and I told him no a bunch of times. It was starting to get creepy, you know, stalky."

"You ever report that to anybody?" I said.

She shook her head.

"Danica," I said, "do you think Eddie could do something like this? Bomb an office?"

She looked at her hands.

"Danny?" Jess said.

She looked at her uncle. Then at her hands again. "He, um, said something to me." She rubbed one thumb with the other. "He said he was going to do something that would blow me away."

"Blow you away?" I said. "Those were his exact words?"

She nodded.

"You think he meant the bomb?"

She shrugged.

"Does anybody else know he said this to you?" I asked.

She shook her head.

"The prosecutor hasn't questioned you?"

Head shake.

I said, "How about Grover Hawthorne?"

That snapped her eyes wide open. A good poker player she wasn't.

"Want to tell me about it?" I said.

She jumped to her feet. "I just want to be left alone!"

She ran into the house.

"She came up here to be with me awhile," Jess said.

"Did she tell you about Grover Hawthorne?" I said.

"No. Who is he?"

"A lawyer. Last week I was eating lunch with my wife at a place called Casa Medina."

"I know it. Played Little League with their kid."

"Danica came in and sat for awhile. Then this guy in a suit

came in and talked to her. I thought that was worth further investigation. I found out he's a lawyer in the office of a lawyer named McCracken."

"McCracken. I know that bird. He sued the ranch once for a slip-and-fall. He lost."

"Think you can convince Danica to talk to me?"

"I'm not gonna force her."

"Does Travis know she's here?"

He shook his head. "He knows Danny and me have always been close."

"If she does open up, would you mind giving us a call?" I took out an Ira law card and put it on the table.

"I won't let her be hurt," he said.

"I don't want that, either," I said. "I just want the truth."

"Guess you do," he said. "Says so on your arm."


An hour-and-a-half later, I pulled into the Somber Sloth and saw Ira's van parked in the lot. I bounded up the stairs like a kid at Christmas.

Ira and Sophie were sitting at the little table in the room.

"Welcome back," Ira said. Ah, that voice. Ira the counselor, Ira the wise, Ira the comfort with his wild spray of gray hair and walrus mustache. He looks like your favorite uncle. When he's with you, you feel like the world has a chance to make sense.

"How do you like the place?" I said.

"Lovely," Ira said. "I've got the room below you."

"Where I can keep an eye on you," I said.

"Sit down. Tell me about Fresno."

I told him. Ira nodded occasionally, sorting facts in his head and putting them in the right folders.

When I finished, Ira said, "What's your little man tell you about Danica possessing evidence that's helpful to us?"

"Fifty-fifty chance," I said. "But we'll never know unless her uncle can convince her to share it, and my read is that's ninety-ten against."

"I still hold out hope for her," Sophie said.

I said, "Based on what?"

She patted my cheek. "I have a little woman inside me."

Ira said, "Shall we talk about the prelim?"

"And then we eat," I said.

"Here's how it will go," Ira said. "The prosecution will present an investigator to detail the police work, and an arson investigator to explain the crime scene. And then he'll put on Santiago Cruz, the only witness who can tie Eddie to the bombing. We'll be ready for him. I've got the slides ready on Miss Daisy."

"Miss Daisy?" Sophie said.

"His laptop," I said.

"I drive her hard," Ira said. "She doesn't let me down. Now, the judge is Honoré Mendoza. Fifty-five, been on the bench twelve years. Graduated from Washburn University School of Law in Topeka. Spent ten years in the D.A.'s office in San Diego. His reputation is he's tough but fair. So no nonsense, Michael."

"Me?" I said.

"You. We're going to try and get this dismissed, not an easy task. The last thing we need is an annoyed judge."

"Yes, boss," I said. "Anything else?"

"Now we may dine," he said.

W e went to Gussie's Diner. Maria was serving. I introduced her to Ira, and asked about her father.

"He's doing better," she said. "Your presence here has given him a shot in the arm, better than anything he gets at the hospital. He's rooting for you."

"That makes it about half a dozen," I said.

"More than you know, I think," she said.

Ira updated us on the Armando Molina case. More and more it was coming down to whether our witness in Los Banos would testify.

"I hope she's still praying," Ira said.

"God parted the Red Sea," I said. "I'm sure he can get through to a frightened widow."

"He has ways," Ira said. "Do you recall the story of Balaam's ass?"

"Are you saying she needs to hear from a talking donkey?" I said.

"You've already seen her," Ira said.

Sophie almost spat out a mouthful of mashed potatoes.

Next morning was damp and drizzly, but not much relief from the heat. We arrived at the courthouse where a knot of reporters buzzed around like bees at a honey pot.

A couple of the bees saw us coming and stepped our way. The others followed. They made with the questions. Ira stopped. He walks with braces due to a bullet he took when he was Mossad. He lifted a hand for silence.

"My name is Ira Rosen, counsel for Mr. Hastings. This is a preliminary hearing, to determine if there's enough evidence to move forward with a trial. Mr. Hastings is presumed innocent. The prosecution must present evidence to show there's a reasonable basis to believe the defendant may have, and I emphasize *may have*, committed the crime. It is not a trial, nor is it any final adjudication. The judge will make the decision whether to move this forward. We have no further comment."

That did not satisfy the bees. They continued peppering Ira with questions but Ira, stoic as a Sphinx, moved through them.

One of the reporters, the same woman from Channel 7

who'd nabbed me when I first saw Eddie at the jail, stepped in front of me.

"What do you think, Mr. Romeo?" she said.

"I think, therefore I am," I said.

Her look was either confused or annoyed, but I was happy either way.

W hen the courtroom doors opened, the buzzing crowd flowed in like sucklings seeking sow's milk. Sophie managed to find a seat before the clerk stopped further inflow.

Ira and I took our place at the defense table. At the other table sat the prosecutor, one Sanford Styles. He was probably in his forties but looked ten years older. He wore horn-rimmed glasses and was dressed like a bored accountant.

Ira hooked up Miss Daisy to the central system. I put his briefcase on the table. Ira took out a couple of file folders and a legal pad.

Then Judge Mendoza came in. He was short and square-shouldered. His face was stone cold. The clerk told everybody to rise and come to order.

The judge sat, we sat, and he said, "Before we begin I want to make it very clear that any disturbance, verbal or otherwise, will be dealt with swiftly and without hesitation. That deputy over there will escort you out and deny you re-entrance. And if I hear a phone go off, may God have mercy on your soul."

With that, he called the matter of the People v. Edward Hastings.

The bailiff opened the side door and called out, "Hastings." A moment later, another deputy came in with Eddie, wearing handcuffs and jailhouse blues. He guided him to the defense table where Ira and I were, and sat him in the chair on my right.

He looked like he hadn't slept in days.

I gave him a pat on the arm. He didn't respond.

Styles wasted no time in the examination of his first two witnesses—an investigator and an arson expert on the bomb details. The story was that Eddie had made a bomb with a timer, accessed the office through a back door, planted it and left. Without being noticed.

Ira only asked a few questions on cross. We knew the People's theory of the case depended completely on the testimony of a single witness, Santiago Cruz. Who was Styles's final witness.

He'd been well prepped. Styles walked him through the details. Cruz answered carefully, using only single sentences. In other words, not going off script.

After ten minutes, Styles said, "That's all I have, Your Honor."

Judge Mendoza looked at Ira. "You may cross examine."

"Good morning, Mr. Cruz," Ira said.

Cruz said nothing.

Ira tapped Miss Daisy. A Google maps image appeared on the mounted screen behind the witness.

"Now, Mr. Cruz, I'd like you to take a look at this picture."

Cruz was able to look at it on a small monitor in front of him.

Ira said, "This is shot from above the street where your shop is located. A red arrow indicates your store. Does that look accurate to you?"

Cruz bent forward. "Yeah."

"And across the street, a blue arrow points to the office of The Central Valley Dispatch. Is that correct?"

"Yeah."

"Now, with the pointer, please turn and indicate on the screen where you were when you saw the car."

Cruz picked up the pointer and fumbled with it.

"Help him out," the judge said to his clerk. The clerk

stepped over to the witness and showed him how to turn on the pointer. Then he instructed Cruz to get out of the chair and point the laser dot at the screen.

Cruz pointed to his store and said, "Right there."

"You were outside or inside?"

"Inside."

"Looking out the window?"

"Yeah."

"You may resume your seat," Ira said, "I am now placing a red dot on the exhibit to mark the spot."

A keystroke later, the dot appeared.

"Is that correct?" Ira said.

"Yeah."

"All right. Now, do you recall talking with my investigator, Mr. Romeo?"

"Yeah."

"He came to your store, is that correct?"

"Yeah."

"And he asked you about what you saw?"

"Yeah."

"And you told Mr. Romeo you saw his car, referring to my client, Mr. Hastings, that you saw his car, in your words, right in front of the office?"

Cruz hesitated. "I don't remember."

"You said essentially the same thing to Mr. Styles, didn't you?"

"Yeah."

"You had the presence of mind to jot down the license plate of the car, yes?"

"It was kind of suspicious, so yeah."

"Being a good citizen, is that it?"

"Sure. Anybody would've."

Ira reached for a document. "May I have the witness look at the police incident report, Your Honor?"

"Hand it to the clerk," the judge said. Ira did so and the clerk took it to the witness.

"Directing your attention to the first page," Ira said. "Do you see where it says incident number?"

Cruz looked at it. "Yeah."

"And do you see where it says nature of the call?"

"Yeah."

"And what does it say was the nature of the call?"

"Heard explosion," Cruz said.

"Below that it says caller. Do you see that?"

"Yeah."

"There's a phone number listed. Do you see that?"

"Yeah."

"That's not your phone number, is it?"

Cruz shook his head.

"Answer Yes or No," the judge said.

"No."

"No further questions," Ira said.

I was surprised by that. He didn't tighten the noose around Cruz's neck.

Judge Mendoza asked Styles if he had any re-direct. Styles said no, and the judge called a fifteen minute recess.

The bailiff escorted Eddie back to the lockup.

"Why didn't you nail him?" I asked Ira.

"Patience, dear boy. We have what we need. Are you ready to testify?"

"I was born ready," I said.

"Don't get cocky. And just answer my questions, okay?"

"Yes, boss."

I went to the rail. Sophie came to me.

"I'm up next," I said.

"Are you ready?"

"I was b…I'm ready."

"You look marvelous," she said. "I hope the sketch artist captures the real you."

"Only you and Ira know the real me," I said.

"I'm still working on that," she said. "But I love my work."

The proceedings were brought back to order by Judge Mendoza.

Ira call me to the stand. I took the oath and sat down.

"Mr. Romeo, you work as my investigator, correct?"

"And I love my work," I said.

Ira shot me a scowl. "You can answer with a simple yes or no."

"Yes."

"You heard the testimony of Mr. Cruz?"

"Yes."

"And was his testimony in accord with your own memory of that conversation?"

"Almost."

"Tell us please, in your own words, about that conversation."

"Mr. Cruz told me that he saw the car right in front of the office."

"His exact words?"

"Right in front, he said. I remember that explicitly, and wrote it down later. I asked him if he saw whoever it was with the bomb, and he said he did not. He said he heard the explosion."

"Did anyone else hear this exchange?"

"Yes, my wife."

"She was with you?"

"Yes."

"So if Mr. Cruz were to later change his testimony, say,

because he said he made a mistake, you and your wife would both be able to flag that change?"

"Objection!" Styles said. "Calls for speculation."

"I'll allow it," the judge said.

"Absolutely," I said.

"I have nothing further," Ira said.

The judge said, "Cross examine?"

"Give me a moment, your honor," Styles said. He leaned over and whispered to his investigator. It was fun to watch.

Finally, Styles said, "No questions."

"The witness may step down," said Judge Mendoza.

I rejoined Ira and Eddie at the defense table.

"Anything else to offer, Mr. Rosen?" the judge said.

"Nothing else," Ira said. "The defense moves the court to dismiss the charge and order the immediate release of Mr. Hastings."

"On what grounds?"

"On the following," Ira said. He tapped his computer and brought back up the photo that had been marked. "According Mr. Cruz, he looked across the street and saw the car parked, lengthwise, in front of the newspaper office. He then stepped away and some time subsequent, heard the explosion. There is no way Mr. Cruze could have seen the license plate of a car parked along the street in front of him. Perjured testimony is no basis for a prosecution."

"Objection!" Styles stood, his face pink.

"Easy does it," the judge said. "Do you have anything else, Mr. Rosen?"

"No, Your Honor. Submitted."

"Mr. Styles?"

Once again, Styles conferred with his investigator. You could have heard a pin drop or a check bounce.

Finally, Styles stood. "Your Honor, we would request a continuance until tomorrow."

"Denied," the judge said. "Anything else?"

"No, Your Honor."

"We'll take a ten-minute recess." He stood and walked off to his chambers.

"What's going on?" Eddie said. "Am I gonna walk?"

"We wait for the judge," Ira said.

"But he has to agree, doesn't he?"

"We wait."

Eddie trembled. I put my hand on his arm. "You're in good hands."

He dropped his head and took a deep breath. The bailiff took him to the lockup.


I was happy. I was confident. I was looking forward to packing up and going home. Sophie and I would head to the beach and play in the waves. C Dog, my young friend in Paradise Cove, would come down and toss a Frisbee with us. The sun would be shining, and the smell in the air would be the cleansing breath of the sea. The unfinished business of poisoned cows, sketchy cops, sketchier politicians, mysterious lawyers, and billionaires with a God complex could all be left behind.

Unless my rattletrap mind couldn't let them go. No easy task. As much as I try to control my brain, my brain holds sway over me. I need to fit things together, pieces of the puzzle, even the universal puzzle of existence.

Like old Heraclitus, I sit on the bank of life with my feet in the water, knowing no one steps in the same river twice. Yet I still want to stop the flow, mark down answers, carve them on stone tablets. Maybe I have a Moses complex. Maybe I'm not so different from Caleb Crane after all. Except for the jet and the money, of course.

. . .

The judge came back in twenty minutes. He wasted no time.

"The court finds probable cause to bind the defendant over for trial. Let's set a date."

Eddie grabbed my arm. "What's going on?"

"Easy," I whispered.

"Why is this happening?"

Mendoza slapped the bench. "Mr. Hastings, do not speak."

"I didn't do it," Eddie said.

"Mr. Rosen, control your client."

Ira leaned toward Eddie. "Let me handle this, Eddie."

I put my arm around our client. He was trembling all over, a wire buzzing with too much current.

Behind me, somebody said, "Give him a kiss."

To his bailiff, Mendoza said, "Take that man out of my courtroom!"

The wise guy, a farmer type who was old enough to know better, got up before the big bailiff reached him and scurried toward the door.

"And you are barred from this courtroom," Mendoza said. "Do not come back, ever."

With that, order was restored, and silence, too, except for Eddie, weeping into his hands.

"Let's set a trial date," Mendoza said.

"Your Honor," Ira said. "We do not waive our right to a speedy trial under 1382."

"Mr. Styles?"

"Fine," Styles said.

"All right," said the judge. "Defendant does not waive his right under Penal Code 1382, and the court finding no good cause for delay, trial will be set within sixty days."

He looked at calendar and gave a date that both counsel agreed to. Fifty-five days from now.

. . .

W e threaded our way through the news hounds outside and made it to Ira's van. I suggested we stop for some Mexican food and bring it back to the Sloth. This we did and ate in Ira's room.

"And so we prepare for trial," Ira said.

"Tell me," I said. "Why didn't you ask Cruz to explain why he didn't call 9-1-1?"

Ira put his burrito on the napkin on his lap, and assumed his rabbi posture. We were about to be taught.

"There are two cardinal rules of cross-examination, my lad," Ira said. "One is never ask an open-ended question, giving the witness wiggle room. Cruz could have made something up, like he was scared or in shock. Leaving the answer where it was gave us another peg upon which the judge could hang a dismissal. But apparently he was dead set against pegs."

"What's the second rule?" Sophie asked.

"Never ask the one question too many," Ira said. "There's an old story, told in law schools and trial workshops for at least a hundred years. There was a defendant on trial for biting off the victim's nose. The sole eyewitness was cross-examined, and the lawyer said, 'You did not see my client bite off the victim's nose, did you?' And the witness answered, 'No.' The lawyer should have left it there. Instead, breaking both cardinal rules, he asked, 'Then how do you know he did it?' And the witness said, 'I saw him spit it out.'"

Sophie laughed. "Good point."

"Jury selection is going to be dicey," Ira said. "We have a jury pool infected with ill feelings toward Eddie. Rooting that out is going to be no easy task. In truth, no one picks a jury. One unpicks a jury. The panel is called and twelve are seated for voir dire."

"To speak the truth," I said.

"Which is rare these days," Ira said. "Jurors who want to get out of the duty will lie. Jurors who want a chance to hang a fellow will lie. Witnesses lie, as we've seen. That's why we have cross-examination. It is the great equalizer for the truth, if conducted properly."

"Like Perry Mason," I said.

Ira chortled. "Unlike Perry Mason. Though I enjoy that show when I want to rest my brain, it is pure fantasy. Perry hammers a witness on the stand so mercilessly that someone in the gallery stands up and confesses. Ha! Nothing good comes from ruthless hammering, though it is a staple of courtroom dramas. The skilled trial lawyer uses a velvet scalpel, quietly eliciting what he needs from a witness and then sitting down, saving the admission for his closing argument, when it's too late for the witness to wiggle out of it."

"He's very good," Sophie said to me.

"He has his moments," I said.

"That wasn't so hard to say, now was it?" Ira said.

By the time we finished our meal, the sun was starting its downward arc. I considered it symbolically. We were going to finish our work here at some point. A couple of months until trial. Ira would head back to L.A., and Sophie, too, as school would soon be in session. I'd hang around for a few days, see Eddie, then drive back to L.A. for a break. Not a happy prospect, but it was my job. And at least I had the rest of this day to hang out with the two people I love most.

I actually felt a moment of peace.

It only took an hour for it to blow up.

W e gathered in Ira's room and went over trial strategy. We discussed the evidence, the vulnerabilities.

"Are you going to put Eddie on the stand?" I asked.

"No," Ira said. "He's too vulnerable."

"Even if he tells the truth?" Sophie said.

"Even so, my dear. It's how the truth is told that matters. In Eddie's state it's too much of a risk. That means we—"

Ira's phone buzzed. He answered and mostly listened.

He put the phone down. "The prosecutor wants to see me."

"When?" I said.

"Now."

"What for?"

"Mr. Styles did not say," said Ira. "Perhaps to discuss a plea deal."

"We won't accept any deal, right?"

"We'll have to consider it."

Sophie said, "But why? He's innocent."

"It's the right question," Ira said. "Any time you go to trial, there's a chance of conviction. And if a deal has been rejected, the judge will sentence the defendant to the maximum penalty. You have to weigh that possibility against your confidence that you can prevail."

"Eddie won't make it in prison," I said. "Let's go tell Styles where he can shove his deal."

"Not we," Ira said.

"I want to be there," I said. "I want to watch his weasel face."

Sophie put her hand on my arm. "You need to stay here."

"She's right," Ira said.

"You're ganging up on me," I said.

"That's clearly what it takes," Ira said.

"How about a game of chess?" Sophie said after Ira left.

"You think you're ready for me?" I said.

"I'll play white," she said.

She opened with e4. I countered with c5, the Sicilian Defense.

Sophie gave me a good game. I mated her on the eighteenth move.

"Rematch," she said.

This time she pushed the Queen's pawn, and I played the Nimzo-Indian Defense favored by Bobby Fischer. This was a more complicated game, and Sophie held her own for an hour and a half.

We were heading for the endgame when Ira came back.

"Things are worse," he said.

He sat at the table and took a couple of documents from his briefcase. He put one on the table. "Medical Examiner's report. Bill Peale's skull shows blunt force trauma. He was dead or dying when the bomb went off."

He tossed the other document. "Forensics report," Ira said. "They searched Eddie's car. The trunk had trace evidence."

"Of what?" I said.

"PETN," Ira said. "Pentaerythritol tetranitrate. An explosive."

"Oh, no," Sophie said.

"Bogus," I said. "Styles just happened to come up with this now?"

"He said the report just came in," Ira said. "But he being generous has offered a deal. Plead guilty and they'll drop the special circumstances. Instead of life without parole, they'll give Eddie twenty-five to life, with parole possible."

I got up so fast I bumped the table and the chess pieces scattered. "This is a pure set up, a plant, a small-town grift! Did you do what I told you? Tell him where to shove it?"

"Keep a cool head," Ira said. "Sit down."

"No."

Sophie got up. She took my arm and sat us on the edge of Ira's bed.

"I can't reject a deal without discussing it with our client," Ira said. "That's the law and the ethics code."

"Ethics." I spat the word.

"Now is just the time to adhere to them," Ira said. "Lest we descend to the lower depths."

"That's where all the action is," I said.

Sophie poked me on the shoulder. "Silence."


I didn't sleep well that night. Sophie did her best nuzzling, but it didn't help the churn inside me. The old Romeo, the pre-Sophie Romeo, was making moves. I got up a little after midnight, sat in a chair and tried to read on my phone. The words scrambled, bumping against thoughts of corruption and monied interests and killers on the loose.

After half an hour I put the phone down. I got my pillow from the bed. I looked at my wife. She was breathing softly.

Don't blow it now, Romeo, like you have so many times. For whatever reason, life handed you a lifeline to the good, the true, and the beautiful. Don't ever do anything to lose her.

I tossed the pillow on the carpet and laid down, looked up at the ceiling, a sea of darkness and merciless silence. When sleep finally came it was on cat's paws, but the cat was a lion with a gaping mouth.


The next morning we said our goodbyes.

Sophie kissed me.

Ira did not.

"Keep your head clear and your blood cool," Ira said.

"You know me," I said.

"Which is why I'm telling you," he said. "Don't become the story."

"If I do, I'll try to make it a short story."

After they drove off I went up on the roof and walked around for awhile. I went back to the room, put on gym shorts, went to the pool and swam a few laps.

A guy came into the pool area with a little boy about three. He had a beard. The man, not the boy.

"How's the water?" the man asked.

"Acceptable," I said.

He took off his T-shirt and flip-flops and brought his boy to the steps. The boy kept looking at me suspiciously. I couldn't blame him.

"What's his name?" I asked.

"Jason," the dad said.

"Good, classic name. Jason and the Argonauts."

"The what?"

"Jason the hero, in search of the Golden Fleece with his crew aboard the ship Argo."

The guy nodded tentatively. "It was my grandfather's name."

"Nice," I said.

The boy was in the water up to his waist. He was smiling now, slapping the water. Pure happiness. In the movie Jason has to kill the hydra, the beast with nine heads. Someday that boy was going to face hydras of his own, as we all do.

I shook the guy's hand and managed to get a high five from Jason. I needed that.

After a shower I spent some time doodling a mind map. It had all the relevant names, and I was drawing lines connecting them as I could. I used a dotted line for a connection I wasn't sure about.

Most lines were dotted.

I was mid-doodle when Jamie Anderson called.

"How's the leg?" I said.

"Okay, I guess. Could have been a lot worse. Missed a vein by a hair."

"Thank God."

"I called to tell you I got into our cloud backup and found a folder called News Backup."

"That was on one of the thumb drives, password protected."

"I cracked it."

"How?"

"Mr. Peale told me once his favorite quote for a newspaper man was 'Comfort the afflicted, and afflict the comfortable.'"

"Reinhold Niebhur," I said.

"Excuse me?"

"Theologian," I said. "He said it. He was a favorite of my mom's."

"Cool. When I was working on a story, Mr. Peale used to tell me 'Afflict 30.'"

"Thirty?"

"That's the old newspaper code for the end of a story. So I tried Afflict30. Didn't work. But then I added the dashes that go before and after the 30, and *that* did it."

"That is some good old-school hacking," I said.

"I'm not going to argue with you," Jamie said. "I found a document in there with various notes. And get this. He was indeed working on a story about Baldwin Fish. He had notes about politics and beef and the McCracken law firm. He thought there was a plot emerging to force Rendell Ranch out of business. One of the notes was titled 'Fish' and referenced a phone interview that he marked as 'Not forthcoming.'"

"No details?"

"Not in that document," Jamie said. "And I couldn't find another doc on point. But the not-forthcoming doc was last updated five days before the bombing."

"Email that material to me," I said.

"Sure. You think Fish is behind it all?"

"Starting to look that way," I said. "I had my own not-very-forthcoming convo with Mr. Fish."

"Oh?"

"Had dinner at Mary Lou's house, Sophie and I. Fish showed up, uninvited. He had an email somebody sent from the Drake library, a threat saying more cows were going to die, and he had to do something about it. I think it was fake."

"Fake?"

"To throw me off the scent, as they say."

"Is there any way we can prove it?" Jamie said.

"I'd love to get Fish alone in a room," I said.

"Maybe I could try to set up an interview."

"You've got a target on your back," I said. "Let me see what I can do on my own."

"But you've got a target on your back, too."

"Yeah, but I'm used to it," I said.


In the afternoon I went to see Eddie at the jail. They brought him to the interview room. His condition was not good. They'd told him he was going to be moved to a medium security prison fifteen miles away. You could almost see the life being sucked out of him.

"I'm scared, Mike" Eddie said. "What'll happen to me? They do things to you in prison."

"Don't fold now," I said. "You can do this. Your first battle is up here." I tapped my head. "You've got three parts—a mind, a heart, and a body. Your mind is the boss. Tell yourself not to give up."

"I can't," he said.

"You have a mouth, right? Open it and tell me you're not giving up."

He shook his head.

"Say it, Eddie," I said. "Say, I'm not giving up."

"I…I don't feel it."

"Make your brain open your mouth and say, I'm not giving up."

He frowned.

I slapped the table. "Say it."

In a barely audible voice he said, "I'm not giving up."

"Good. Now say it like you mean it."

"But I don't mean it."

"Say it *like* you mean it."

"This is stupid."

"Don't bail on me now," I said. "Or on Ira, or Sophie. We're in this together and you owe us that much. Just one time. Say it like you mean it."

He hung his head. I thought he was through. But then he raised it and said, "I'm not giving up."

"Better," I said. "Say it to yourself a hundred times a day. Will you do that for me?"

"Okay," he said.

It was a start.


A t the front desk I asked about the status of Dante Hooker.

The guy didn't respond.

"Anytime," I said.

He shook his head.

"Use language," I said.

"Nothing to say," he said.

"Why not?"

"You're not next of kin."

Little rockets went off inside me. "He's dead?"

"That's all I have to say."

"This is a public jail," I said. "You can't withhold information like this."

"I can."

"Who's in charge here?"

"I am," he said.

"Perfect," I said.


I raced back to the Sloth and called Sophie.

"I just saw Eddie. He's on the edge. I'm going to have to see him a lot to keep him from falling off. But get this. That guy I found at Bill Peale's house, Dante. He's dead."

"What? How?"

"They're not saying, at least not to me. But if this is one of those he-hanged-himself-in-his-cell type deals, it stinks to high heaven."

"Oh, Mike, what is going on?"

"I better find out, and soon."

"I want to be there with you."

"Tell me something normal," I said. "Everything okay at home?"

"C Dog dropped by. He's very serious about his girlfriend. And he's reading a book."

"Comic book?"

"No, an actual book he got from the library."

"He went to the library?"

"All by himself," Sophie said.

"What's the book?"

"A history of 80s hard rock."

"Ah, he's reading history. I'll give him Gibbon next."

"You'll break him," Sophie said.

"Just Volume One."

"Let me do the suggesting," she said.

"It will be a team effort," I said.

We talked a few more minutes about gloriously mundane things—what she was having for dinner, what her lesson plans were, what to do for Ira's birthday. I embraced the quietness of it.

Then the call was over. I looked at the four walls.

*I better find out, and soon.*

Joey Feint used to say "If at first you don't succeed, sniff, sniff again." Go over everything you know, revisit all the dead ends, shake the trees once more. It's the grunt work that makes up most of the investigatory task.

I started to make a list of unanswered questions. When I got to seven I stopped. That was more than enough to sniff.

First on my list was Danica Rendell.

I called Jess.

"Any further word on Danica talking to me?" I asked.

"Sorry, no."

"Would you tell her a couple of things for me? Tell her Dante Hooker is dead. He was arrested and jailed and croaked. I couldn't get the details, but it's either a suicide or made to look like it."

"Crazy."

"Tell Danica I'm trying to keep Eddie from the same thing. Tell her if she knows anything at all, now's the time, before it's too late."

"I'll try," Jess said. "But I can't promise anything."

"That's all I ask."

Next on my list was looking at the docs Jamie sent me from the cracked News_Backup file. I started with the doc called "Fish." It opened with biographical notes.

*Born, raised Visalia. Family farm.*
*U.C. Berkeley. Poli-Sci. Crew.*
*Environmental causes.*
*Tulare County Board of Supervisors.*
*Single.*

Then notes about Peale's phone interview five days before his murder.

*Questions:*
*Connection with McCracken firm?*
*Rendell Ranch litigation?*
*Not forthcoming.*

That was it. He was being careful with these notes. A story pulsated beneath the surface. But what was it? No big reveal.

In frustration I looked at the folders from the other thumb drive. I decided to be methodical and look at everything.

I started with the Memoir folder. One document, 55 pages. I read the opening.

*I've spent over forty years chasing deadlines, on typewriters in a small-town newsroom to computers in a world that doesn't slow down for anybody. I started as a wide-eyed kid, thinking I'd change the world with passion and words. Instead, the world changed me. But not so much that I've forgotten where I came from or what a newspaper's supposed to do—tell the story, plain and true, no matter what it costs.*

Yeah, and it cost Bill Peale everything. I sped through the rest. It would've made a good read. But nothing that helped my cause.

I almost didn't look at the Novel folder. But just to cover all bases, I opened it. It was only fifteen pages. The title was *Against This Land.*

*The road curved with the land, rising gently until it opened into a valley. He pulled the truck to the side and stepped out into the silence. The air carried the sharp bite of sage and dust, the kind of scent that rooted a man to the earth.*

Not bad. I quick-scanned the rest of it. The setting was a Montana ranch. The protagonist, Cal Tucker, was worried about a legal battle for his ranch. A slick gubernatorial candidate offered his help, but had other interests.

Didn't take a Rhodes Scholar to figure this to be a *roman à clef* about Travis Rendell and Baldwin Fish.

And one other character.

Which made my head explode.

I rapped on the door. No answer. I knocked again.

The door opened.

"Mike, what a surprise," Mary Lou said.

"I need your help, Mary Lou," I said.

"Help?"

"Can I come in?"

"I was just getting ready to go out."

"This won't take long. It concerns Eddie Hastings."

"Oh, well, certainly. Come in."

We went into the living room. We didn't sit down.

"How can I help?" Mary Lou said.

"As you know, Eddie is sitting in a jail cell, waiting to go on trial for murder."

"Yes, I know. I'm sorry, Mike."

"You can help me set him free."

"Me? How?"

"Bill Peale was working on a novel. It was based on Rendell Ranch."

"Really?"

"He'd barely started it, but the characters bear a striking resemblance to Travis Rendell and Baldwin Fish."

"That's so wild."

"There was a third character, a woman, who bore a unique nickname. He called her A1."

Her mouth quivered.

I said, "Isn't that what Travis calls you?"

The stillness in the room was like an empty cathedral.

"You poisoned the cows, didn't you?"

"Mike!" She put her hand on her chest. "Why would you say that?"

"Because you're in love with Travis Rendell. You thought if you manufactured a crisis at the ranch, he'd come to realize how much he needed you."

"Mike, you can't possibly—"

"Bill Peale found out about it, went to Baldwin Fish with it. Asked some questions Fish didn't like. According to the plot, A1 was sleeping with the Fish character."

Mary Lou's girl-boss facade began to crack like ice on a frozen lake getting that first blast of Spring sun.

"You were using Fish," I said. "Or was it the other way around? All that fake animosity between you two."

"Mike, wait—"

"Fish told you about Bill Peale's interview, didn't he? And that's why you both wanted him dead."

"Mike, you don't know what's going on." Her voice was a low tremble. "You don't know…"

"Go ahead and fill me in."

A voice said, "Forget it, Mary Lou."

Into the room stepped the cop, Jacobsen.

Holding a shotgun.

Pointed at me.


The shotgun was single-barrel, break-action. Held only one load. Not a cop gun, which would have been pump-action and held more rounds. My grandfather had a shotgun. He lived on a farm in Indiana and once showed me what a shotgun could do to a serried row of tin cans. Boom! I knew from his instruction that even from twenty feet away, buckshot doesn't spread all that much. It stays in a tight cluster about the size of dinner plate.

More than enough to make spaghetti of my insides.

"I didn't see a cop car out there," I said. "This won't be logged as official business."

Jacobsen smiled. "Mary Lou is my friend. Aren't you, Mary Lou?"

Mary Lou said nothing.

I said, "You bring a shotgun to see friends?"

"This is Mary Lou's," Jacobsen said. "She's quite the cowgirl."

"Hold on, Mark," Mary Lou said.

"Shut up," Jacobsen said. "He broke in and you shot him. Get out of the way."

"Don't fall for it, Mary Lou," I said.

Mary Lou's longhorn steer statuette looked at me from the end table.

Five feet away.

Mary Lou took a step toward Jacobsen. "Just think."

"Look out," Jacobsen said.

I lunged right, grabbed the steer.

Jacobsen shouted, "Move!" and lurched left.

I dove and side-armed the steer.

*Boom!*

Hot claws ripped my shoulder and deltoid.

There would be blood.

But the shotgun was spent.

I rolled, got up, ran at Jacobsen.

He raised the gun to smash my head with it.

I ducked and hit him like a tackling dummy. We slammed against the wall.

My shoulder burned.

Jacobsen gun-butted my back but the blow was weak.

I drove my head up into his chin and felt the crunch. I brought my arms up inside his and pushed out.

He dropped the shotgun.

He must have done some wrestling in his time. He over-hooked my left arm and fresh fire scorched my shoulder. He hooked my leg and twisted his hips.

I hit the floor like a cinder block, Jacobsen on top of me, pinning my good arm. My ribs bent inward like bony clamps, crushing out my air.

He pounded a right to my jaw. I tasted blood. That taste gave me a jolt. I managed to get my bad wing up. I claw-gripped his throat. But I knew I wasn't strong enough to finish him.

He choked out a laugh. Spittle sprayed my face.

And there we were in complete lockup. Face to face, animal to animal. Like Buck and Spitz in *The Call of the Wild*. This was the law of club and fang. To the death. A swirl of black began to spin in the far reaches of my brain, approaching, growing like a tornado on a dusty plain. In my mind I screamed *Hang onto the light*!

Where was Mary Lou?

I felt Jacobsen reach for something. A knife?

Then came that desperation you feel when death is suddenly real, breathes on your face, a shroud dropping, and my last thoughts were not of my life flashing before my eyes, but a picture, a portrait, framed in a soft aura of gold— Sophie's face—and a last electric charge went through me, Sophie, Sophie, I thrust my knee into his crotch. It got me a second of weakening in his hold. I pulled my good arm free.

Wildly I reached out, feeling for something, anything—the shotgun, a chair.

What I touched was the statuette.

Jacobsen cursed, jerked his head, and broke free of my left hand.

But not my right. With a last surge of adrenaline I drove the horns of the Texas steer into the neck of Mark Jacobsen.

The spray of blood told me I'd found his carotid artery.

Jacobsen brought his hands to his throat and I pushed him off. The black swirl receded. Light poured in. I got to my knees.

"Mike, move." It was Mary Lou's voice, behind me.

She was holding the shotgun.

"What?" I said.

"It's loaded," she said. "Look out."

"Whoa, whoa."

Jacobsen gurgled on the floor.

"We can make this work." Mary Lou said.

I fought for breath. "Make what work?"

"He's the intruder, see? He came to kill us. We can do this."

"I need to help him," I said.

"No," she said.

Jacobsen stopped moving.

"We can get away with this," she said. "Both of us."

"It won't work," I said. "Too many lies."

"People do it all the time," she said.

"Mary Lou, I've got a client facing a murder charge."

She paused. Then turned the shotgun on me.

"That won't make it go away," I said.

"I won't go to prison," she said.

"You think killing me is going to keep you out?"

"It's…a chance."

I shook my head. "Let me help you. I know the best lawyer in California."

She took a step back. "I won't go."

"It's not the end of your life," I said.

"No, Mike."

"Put the gun down. Let's talk it through."

She took another step back, shaking her head.

"You know this isn't right," I said.

She kept the shotgun on me, quivering. A twitch would spasm her trigger finger and it would be goodbye Romeo.

There were tears in her eyes.

"Take your finger off the trigger, Mary Lou."

For a long moment she didn't move, except for her arms shuddering.

She dropped her hand.

"That's it," I said.

Then she flipped the shotgun and put the barrel under her chin.

"Mary Lou, no!"

She reached down with her right hand, thumb extended toward the trigger.

"That's not the way," I said. "It's never the—"

*Boom!*

I went to the bathroom and took off what was left of my shirt and put it in the sink. I grabbed a towel, wet it, wiped away blood on my face and chest, and pressed it to my shoulder.

I took out the card Officer Tanner gave me. I called him and told him to come to the house on the double.

"Tell me why," he said.

"There's blood and a dead body," I said.

I clicked off.

On the sofa, Mary Lou was weeping into her hands. She'd started crying before she moved the barrel from under her chin, but not her thumb from the trigger. Her living room ceiling was going to need a lot of work.

I sat next to her. She put her head on my shoulder, the good one.

"I'm sorry, Mary Lou," I said.

"I know," she said.

"You'll have to tell them everything."

She nodded.

"Let me help you," I said. "It'll be hard, but I'll help you."

She wiped her eyes with the back of her hand. "When you do wrong, make it right, and let the buffalo chips fall where they may."

It was a gasp from a solid past, from a principle handed down from father to daughter, latent, coming out at last to save her soul.

I knew I would never have the heart to reveal that I made up the part about the female character being named A1. It was actually Loretta in Peale's novel.

"Tell me what this is all about," I said.

"Can you help me, Mike? Really?"

"Tell me."

She didn't want to fall in love with Travis Rendell. When his wife died, Mary Lou hated herself for thinking of taking her place. But her love intensified into a kind of madness. She tried to get over it by having an affair with Baldwin Fish.

"The worst decision," she said. "Until the cows."

She thought by poisoning some cows she could show Travis how necessary she was to him, the ranch, the whole enterprise. The way a good ramrod was essential to a trail boss in the days of the cattle drives. Fish knew she was up to something and hired Jacobsen to follow her around. He'd used Jacobsen before to gather dirt on locals.

Fish and Jacobsen confronted her one night and she broke. But Fish told her to relax. He'd "take care" of things.

At the same time somebody else was gathering information —Bill Peale. He made that fateful call to Fish.

That's when Jacobsen went rogue with a good old black-mail scheme against Fish. He kicked it up a notch when he murdered Peale and set up Eddie Hastings with the help of Santiago Cruz, and planted evidence in Eddie's car.

Mary Lou wanted none of it, but it was too late. It was Jacobsen who controlled everything now, and he relished it.

"Did he kill Dante Hooker?" I asked.

"I don't know," she said. "He could have..."

Her voice trailed off. She was spent, leaning against me.

"Quiet now," I said. "Let me do the talking from here on out."

A few minutes later Officers Tanner and Plante came through the front door and into the living room.

"Good God, what happened here?" Tanner said.

"That's Mark Jacobsen," I said.

Officer Plante went over to look.

"Don't step on the blood," I said.

Plante said, "It is Mark."

"Start talking," Tanner said. He had his sidearm out.

"Your boy tried to shred me with that shotgun," I said.

Tanner frowned. "Why is he dead?"

"Listen," I said. "Miss Overstreet is in the care of attorney Ira Rosen and me. She's a material witness to murder. She will not say anything until Mr. Rosen is with us. Right now she is going to lie down."

I stood and helped Mary Lou to her feet.

"Where you going?" Tanner said.

"The bedroom," I said.

"I can't let you do that."

"You can and will," I said. "And get in touch with Gracie. Tell him we're going to deliver him a big fish."

"A what?"

"Tell him that." I took Mary Lou's arm and walked past Tanner. He didn't try to stop us. I don't know what I would have done if he had.

I helped Mary Lou get on her bed. I took off her boots and covered her with the bedspread.

"Just rest now," I said. "I'll be right here."

Tanner was watching from the doorway. "I need to question you. I need to give you Miranda."

"Let's cut it short," I said. "Nobody is saying anything until my lawyer arrives."

That's when I called Ira.

"How soon can you get here?" I said.

"Whoa. What's happening?"

"I can't say much at the moment. There's a very nice police officer standing next to me."

"Are you in custody?"

"Temporarily."

"Michael, what's that—"

"We have our proof. We have the killer. We have a witness, and she needs your help."

I could almost feel Ira's head spinning.

"How soon, Ira?"

"I can be on the road in half an hour," he said.

An hour later Gracie came in with a young guy carrying a leather bag. They took a look at the body, Gracie talked to Tanner, then to me.

"You want to tell me what happened?" he said.

"You got the basics from Officer Tanner."

"I'd like to hear it from you."

"Do this," I said. "Arrange a meeting with DDA Styles. We'll be there, along with my lawyer. Then you'll get the whole thing."

"Officer Tanner said something about a fish."

"A big fish," I said.

"So what's that mean?"

"Set up the meeting."

He scowled. "Let me see your shoulder."

I removed the towel that was draped over it.

Gracie said, "I'll have Vince take a look at it. He can patch you up."

"I'll take it," I said. "There, see? I can get along with law enforcement."

Gracie grunted. But I thought I saw the start of a smile.

The meeting was at the D.A.'s office at one in the afternoon. Styles, Gracie and the head of the office, a guy named Rickard, were present, along with Ira, Mary Lou and me. Ira did his magic act. In return for testifying against Baldwin Fish, Mary Lou would not be charged with conspiracy to commit murder. She would plead guilty to five counts of animal cruelty, with a sentence recommendation of three years probation, restitution, and 200 hours of community service.

She would serve no time in prison.

And Eddie Hastings would be going home.

Ira headed back to L.A. I went to the county prison to get Eddie processed out. He'd lost weight. He looked like a boxer sitting on his stool after getting knocked down at the end of a round—dazed, eyes trying to focus.

We got in Spinoza. I put the top down.

"What now?" Eddie said.

"Let's get your car out of impound," I said.

"I mean, with my life. I don't know if I want to go back to Drake."

"The worst time to make a life decision is after you've just been knocked out. Give yourself a few days, rest up, do something you enjoy. What do you like to do, Eddie?"

He thought about it. "I like movies."

"Want to see a movie right now?"

"Now?"

"Sure."

"You'll come with me?" he said.

"No, you'll come with me," I said.

"What movie?"

"Sergeant York," I said.

"I haven't heard of that one. Who's in it?"

"Gary Cooper."

"Who?"

"You have got some learning to do," I said.

I stopped at an AM/PM and got two big bags of popcorn and a couple of Cokes. I took us to my room, closed the curtains, opened my laptop, and we watched Sergeant York.

When it was over, Eddie was silent for a long moment. Then, in a quiet but awestruck voice he said, "That was the best movie I've ever seen."

"You're gonna be all right, Eddie," I said.

We went to the impound lot and got Eddie's car. I put my hand out to shake goodbye.

Eddie hugged me.

"Can I keep in touch with you?" he said.

"I'd be disappointed if you didn't," I said.

"Thanks for everything."

"Read good books."

He got in his car and drove off, literally into the sunset. It'd be dark soon. I could've spent the night and taken that long drive home in the morning.

Never entered my mind. It took me ten minutes to pack up, check out, and get on the freeway heading south. The cow smell followed me for a mile or so, and then it was gone.

J amie Anderson wrote the story. It got national attention and most local newscasts in California did a feature on it. And why not? Baldwin Fish—once "a rising star in California politics"—indicted for murder and conspiracy to commit murder.

And Danica Rendell had finally talked. Fish had lured her into an affair to groom her as a tool against her father's interests. Grover Hawthorne was the go-between. Now Baldwin Fish was spouting denials about everything, claiming this was all a conspiracy against him.

Yawn. You need a dark, monied villain for a good conspiracy. But no connection has been made to Caleb Crane. He's free to live another hundred years.

Mary Lou Overstreet moved back to the town where she grew up and is living with her sister.

And Eddie Hastings? He sent me an email three weeks after his release.

*Hey Mike, just wanted to tell u I decided what I'm doing. I met with an Army recruiter. I'm going in! Need to put on some weight but I can do that. Stay out of trouble. Eddie.*

Stay out of trouble? Me? No problem.

. . .

A week ago our star witness in the Armando Molina case, Rosario Ramirez, informed me that she would testify in court. Her Lady had told her it was the merciful thing to do. The prosecutor is the one who needs mercy now. When Ira tries a case it's like Dudamel conducting the L.A. Phil. The symphony will be "Rosen's Reasonable Doubt in C Minor," with its final movement, "Not Guilty." I will have a front row seat.

L ast night, Sophie and I sat on our porch listening to the waves caress the sands of Paradise Cove. My left arm was finally out of a sling. My shoulder still yelped every now and then, but I didn't care. I could put both arms around Sophie now when the mood struck me. Which was often.

"How do you like it?" Sophie said.

"Like what?" I said.

"A moment's peace."

"It's nice, I'll admit," I said. "Let's make it last."

"Says Mike Romeo."

"I know. But I've been thinking…"

"Uh-oh."

"Maybe I should stick around home for awhile, be domestic, plant some spring flowers, or maybe…"

"Maybe what?"

I took her hand and kissed it.

"Maybe we should get a cow."

She laughed then, and I loved her laugh. At that moment I knew something beyond a reasonable doubt—beyond any possible doubt, in fact. I knew I needed Sophie like I need blood in my veins and a beating heart.

And that's the God's honest truth.

# AUTHOR'S NOTE

Many thanks for reading *Romeo's Truth*. I greatly appreciate it. Added appreciation would come if you would kindly leave a review on the Amazon site.

**The Mike Romeo Thriller Series**
(in order)
1. Romeo's Rules
2. Romeo's Way
3. Romeo's Hammer
4. Romeo's Fight
5. Romeo's Stand
6. Romeo's Town
7. Romeo's Rage
8. Romeo's Justice
9. Romeo's Fire
10. Romeo's Truth

## FREE BOOK

I'd like to offer you a free suspense novella, FRAMED. You can pick it up by going to my website: JamesScottBell.com. Navigate to the FREE BOOK page and follow the link. Enjoy!

# MORE THRILLERS FROM JAMES SCOTT BELL

**The Ty Buchanan Legal Thriller Series**

#1 Try Dying
#2 Try Darkness
#3 Try Fear

"Part Michael Connelly and part Raymond Chandler, Bell has an excellent ear for dialogue and makes contemporary L.A. come alive. Deftly plotted, flawlessly executed, and compulsively readable. Bell takes his place as one of the top authors in the crowded suspense genre." - **Sheldon Siegel**, *New York Times* bestselling author

**The Complete JSB Short Fiction Collection**

Down These Streets

**The Trials of Kit Shannon Historical Legal Thrillers**

Book 1 - City of Angels

Book 2 - Angels Flight
Book 3 - Angel of Mercy
Book 4 - A Greater Glory
Book 5 - A Higher Justice
Book 6 - A Certain Truth

"With her shoulders squared and faith set high, Kit Shannon arrives in 1903 Los Angeles feeling a special calling to practice law … Packed full of genuine, deep and real characters … The tension and suspense are in overdrive … A series that is timeless!" — **In the Library Review**

**Stand Alone Thrillers**

Can't Stop Me
Your Son Is Alive
Long Lost
No More Lies
Blind Justice
Don't Leave Me
Final Witness
Framed
Last Call

**Mallory Caine, Zombie-At-Law Series**

You read that right. A new genre. Part John Grisham, part Raymond Chandler—it's just that the lawyer is dead. Mallory Caine, Zombie at Law, defends the creatures no other lawyer will touch…and longs to reclaim her real life.

Pay Me In Flesh
The Year of Eating Dangerously
I Ate The Sheriff

# ABOUT THE AUTHOR

**James Scott Bell** is the multi-bestselling author of thrillers, books on the writing craft, and the Substack newsletter Whimsical Wanderings. He is a winner of both the International Thriller Writers Award and the Christy Award (Suspense). He attended the University of California, Santa Barbara, where he studied writing with Raymond Carver, and graduated with honors from USC Law School. He lives and writes in Los Angeles.

JamesScottBell.com
JamesScottBell.substack.com

www.ingramcontent.com/pod-product-compliance
Lightning Source LLC
Chambersburg PA
CBHW020645260626
47157CB00008B/2915